INKED CRAVING

A MONTGOMERY INK: FORT COLLINS NOVEL

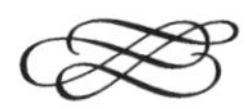

CARRIE ANN RYAN

INKED CRAVING

A Montgomery Ink: Fort Collins Novel

By
Carrie Ann Ryan

Inked Craving
A Montgomery Ink: Fort Collins Novel
By: Carrie Ann Ryan

eBook ISBN: 978-1-950443-68-0
Paperback ISBN: 978-1-950443-69-7

Cover Art by Sweet N Spicy Designs
Photograph by Sara Eirew

INKED CRAVING

The Montgomery Ink saga from NYT Bestselling Author Carrie Ann Ryan continues with a friends to lovers romance that breaks all of their own rules.

Instead of walking away with a marriage proposal, Paige Montgomery ended up broken hearted and pregnant.

Now she has to figure out how to begin her life again alone.

She refuses to fall for another man, yet every time she sees Lee Grier, her traitorous heart aches for him. It doesn't matter he's her brother's best friend and wants to be her rock in the storm. She knows she has to weather the oncoming pressures on her own.

When they can no longer fight the pull between

them, they'll have to remember that passion can only shelter them from reality for so long and letting themselves fall will be the hardest step yet.

PRAISE FOR CARRIE ANN RYAN

“Count on Carrie Ann Ryan for emotional, sexy, character driven stories that capture your heart!” – Carly Phillips, NY Times bestselling author

“Carrie Ann Ryan’s romances are my newest addiction! The emotion in her books captures me from the very beginning. The hope and healing hold me close until the end. These love stories will simply sweep you away.” ~ NYT Bestselling Author Deveny Perry

"Carrie Ann Ryan writes the perfect balance of sweet and heat ensuring every story feeds the soul." - Audrey Carlan, #1 New York Times Bestselling Author

“Carrie Ann Ryan never fails to draw readers in with passion, raw sensuality, and characters that pop off the page. Any book by Carrie Ann is an absolute treat.” – New York Times Bestselling Author J. Kenner

“Carrie Ann Ryan knows how to pull your heartstrings and make your pulse pound! Her wonderful Redwood Pack series will draw you in and keep you reading long into the night. I can’t wait to see what comes next with the new generation, the Talons. Keep them coming, Carrie Ann!” –Lara Adrian, New York Times bestselling author of CRAVE THE NIGHT

"With snarky humor, sizzling love scenes, and brilliant, imaginative worldbuilding, The Dante's Circle series reads as if Carrie Ann Ryan peeked at my personal wish list!" – NYT Bestselling Author, Larissa Ione

"Carrie Ann Ryan writes sexy shifters in a world full of passionate happily-ever-afters." – *New York Times* Bestselling Author Vivian Arend

"Carrie Ann's books are sexy with characters you can't help but love from page one. They are heat and heart blended to perfection." *New York Times* Bestselling Author Jayne Rylon

Carrie Ann Ryan's books are wickedly funny and deliciously hot, with plenty of twists to keep you guessing. They'll keep you up all night!" USA Today Bestselling Author Cari Quinn

"Once again, Carrie Ann Ryan knocks the Dante's Circle series out of the park. The queen of hot, sexy, enthralling paranormal romance, Carrie Ann is an author not to miss!" *New York Times* bestselling Author Marie Harte

PROLOGUE

Paige

Tonight was the night.

After over a year of dating, tonight was the night Colton and I would finally take the next step. He'd called me this morning and asked me to meet him at one of our favorite spots. He'd sounded so nervous and told me that he was excited over something. Colton had sent over flowers the day before with a note saying, 'just because' and I couldn't stop smiling.

Tonight, Colton would get down on one knee and propose to me. And I would say yes.

I loved him with every ounce of my soul and could not wait until we started our life together.

I bit my lip as I looked into the mirror, pinning my hair back from my face. I loved Colton. He made me smile, made me laugh, and I knew I'd spend the rest of my life with him. He was my everything, and I could not wait to say yes.

I wore a light peach wrap-dress, one that I loved and made me happy to wear. I felt pretty and like a princess. Instead of a crown, I had a planner and a tablet, but it worked for me. Just in case tonight *wasn't* the night, I still looked and felt pretty. I was a realist with my head in the clouds for only moments, not the entire day, after all.

With one last look in the mirror, I made my way to my car, singing and dancing in my seat as I drove toward the park. The night was beautiful, with not a cloud in sight. The moon was full, and the sky was bright.

Romance filled the air, and if I were any more jovial and lighthearted, I'd be filled with cotton candy and annoy the hell out of my family.

I smirked as I parked, shaking my head. I was the giddy one of the group, just like Archer, but I probably hit the annoyance factor more. I didn't mind since a grumpy Montgomery was a normal Montgomery. I'd be the weird one.

Hopefully, later tonight, I'd be the *engaged* weird one.

I picked up my bag and did my best not to skip to our meeting spot on the patio outside of Colton's restaurant in the park. We'd met at this spot, and I'd fallen for him at that exact moment.

Montgomerys didn't always fall at first sight, but when they did, it lasted.

I gripped my hands tightly in front of me as Colton came forward, his blond hair messy and pushed back from his face. The ends reached his collar, and while I knew he wanted a haircut, I liked the surfer look on him. He was gorgeous, tan, intelligent, caring, and *mine*.

"Paige."

His voice was smooth whiskey that slid over me, and I couldn't help but smile wide. I loved this man so much, and it almost hurt sometimes because it was too much. I'd never fallen like this before, and I wasn't sure how I was supposed to make clear and coherent thoughts when he was around.

"Colton." I went up to my tiptoes and pressed my lips to his. He was taller than me, so he always had to lean down for me to kiss him. I didn't mind. He always made sure I could have his lips, his taste—his everything.

"I'm glad you could make it. I have a busy shift

tonight but wanted to talk with you about something important and time-sensitive."

I blinked, wondering if this was a different way to begin a proposal. I'd never been proposed to, however, so I wasn't sure.

"I'm here. Thank you so much for inviting me out tonight. I love this spot. It's the first place I met you." My heart raced, and I told myself to calm down.

He blinked, distracted. "That's right. I forgot. I like it because it's so close to the restaurant, so I don't have to take much time away. You know?"

Not really, but maybe I was making too much of his words.

"I'm glad it's close, then."

He smiled. "I have great news, Paige. Do you know Massimo? The chef out in New York that's opening a new place?"

I tilted my head, dread pooling in my belly as my dreams of the evening began to shatter like fine glass all around me. "I remember him."

He'd been a jerk and an egotistical asshole when he'd visited and had treated Colton like something under his shoe, but I didn't mention that part.

"Good! Because he offered me a position. Head fucking chef. He needs someone to do it all. As a *partner*. It won't just be his place, but *ours*. I'll get to work with one of the best, Paige. It's been a dream of mine since I was a kid to own a restaurant in New York and be in the *scene,* and now I finally get my chance. I'm so fucking excited, babe."

I swallowed hard, the ringing in my head growing louder as I tried to keep up. "New York? As in… not in Colorado? What… what are you talking about, Colton?"

He seemed to realize he might have said the wrong thing because he winced before reaching out to cup my face. I took a step back, not sure I wanted him to touch me at that moment. I wasn't sure what I'd say to him if he did.

"Babe."

"Please don't call me babe." I'd never hated it before, but I didn't like it then.

"Paige. This is a great opportunity. Once in a lifetime."

"I thought *we* were once in a lifetime."

He grimaced. "Paige, baby. It's a huge chance—my big break. I mean… I guess you can come with me."

He *guessed.* As in, he wasn't sure. As in, I wasn't at the forefront of his mind.

"My entire family is here, Colton. My job. My life. I can't just move to New York and start another Montgomery Builders. That's not how this works."

He ran his hand through his hair. "Shit. I didn't think you'd react like this."

"How am I supposed to react, Colton? I thought you

were going to fucking propose, and now you're saying you're moving across the country and didn't think about what would happen to me when you did?" I hadn't meant to let all of those words out, and now there was no way to take them back.

Colton blanched. "Paige…it's not that I don't like you. I do."

I held up my hand before he could break my heart any more than he had. "Don't. Don't placate me. Clearly, we were looking at this relationship from very different places. I—I can't look at you right now." I didn't want him to see me break.

"I need to head back, Paige. I can't let them do this without me. We'll talk later. I promise. We'll figure something out."

I met his gaze, grateful that my eyes were dry. "No, don't. It's fine. Go. Just go."

Then he did the only thing he could do, the only thing that broke me. He left. And he didn't look back.

I stood on our spot, grateful for the privacy, but I couldn't breathe. I couldn't think.

I'd thought I'd found my happiness. I thought I was ready for my future.

It turned out I was once again the baby Montgomery with her head in the clouds and stars in her eyes. Colton didn't love me. Colton wasn't my forever.

And somehow, I was supposed to walk away from here as if nothing had happened.

My body began to shake, and I pulled out my phone, knowing I needed someone. I couldn't breathe. I couldn't drive. I needed help.

Only I didn't want to put that on their shoulders. I didn't want to bother them and have them worry about little Paige again. That's all they'd done my entire life.

I rolled my shoulders back and made my way to my car. I'd deal with this alone—just like I should have done in the beginning.

I'd put my faith in the wrong man, and I promised myself I'd never do it again.

The Montgomerys fell hard, and now it seemed they broke even harder.

I'd fallen once, and I vowed to myself even as I fought through the pain, I'd never do it again.

I'd never fall in love with anyone ever again.

No matter what fate tossed my way.

CHAPTER 1

Paige

There were times in my life when I was ready for anything. When I could look at the world in front of me and know that I could handle it. It was what I did. If something went wrong when it came to my business, family, or life, I found a way to make it work. I made it happen.

If I made a mistake, I handled that, too. If I had my heart broken over and over again until I was nothing, I found a way to take it and grow from it.

I could not weather this.

I sat on the edge of the bathtub, my feet in slippers,

my shorts riding up since I had pulled them up too quickly. I hadn't put on a bra, my tank top old and ratty. Yet it was all comfortable. I looked like the epitome of the hot mess I was, but nobody would see this. Other than me and my reflection.

I couldn't remember if I had washed my hair this week, and I was pretty sure my sister had noticed. Considering that I was a whiz with dry shampoo and subtle updos, no one should have seen, but it had been at least since Monday. Showering was something I did daily because I still worked out and needed the hot water on my skin. I couldn't sleep, so I craved something that made me tired.

Yet, something was wrong. Terribly wrong.

I looked down at the stick in my hand, at the five other sticks on the counter, the two more on the floor, and I didn't cry. I didn't do anything. I just sat there and looked down at the words that were clear, evident, and part of the name of the damn brand.

Pregnant.

I, Paige Montgomery, youngest of the Montgomery clan, including all other nineteen or so cousins, was pregnant.

Out of wedlock, out of a relationship, and left behind.

"This cannot be happening." My words echoed in the bathroom, yet it was the truth. Every positive test, whether they be pink, blue, one line, two, an odd assortment of dots, or the clear words that said *pregnant,* let me know I was with child.

Something was growing inside me, taking nutrients and splitting cells and creating an amorphous blob until it would one day be the size of a cantaloupe, and then some other food product that would eventually be compared to an actual baby. And then I would give birth.

I would have a baby.

I scrambled off the edge of the bathtub, threw open the toilet lid, and proceeded to empty my stomach.

I honestly didn't think it had anything to do with morning sickness, but rather…heart sickness.

I was pregnant.

Pregnant with Colton's baby. The same guy who had left me and hadn't taken a second look back after thinking he'd be *so* happy with his new life.

He had known what his life would be and decided to take that job in New York as if that would be his pinnacle of success and identity.

He'd left me, and I had let him. But he hadn't left me alone. No, I was going to have a baby.

I swallowed hard and lay down on the floor as I let the sweat cool, my pants slowly receding as my body quit shaking.

This didn't feel real. Maybe it wasn't. I would have

to go to the doctor. They would likely tell me that there were a bunch of false positives and that it just happened. It was a way of life. That had to be it. Because there was no way I could be pregnant.

I had wanted marriage, a future, all of that—everything that came with being with Colton and starting the next phase of our life. I had wanted all of it, yet it seemed as if I wouldn't get it.

Because I was broken.

I blinked, annoyed with myself for that thought because it was so unlike me. No, I couldn't be broken. Pregnant people couldn't be broken. They had to face the future and deal with the fact that it wasn't only their life that was the center of their universe. And why was I going through a thousand different emotions?

I let out a breath and then looked over at my phone.

I needed to tell Colton. I needed to tell him that we were having a baby.

"No, *I'm* having a baby." He'd left us. He wanted nothing to do with this life and was already having a carefree time with the perfect job and the perfect future in New York. He hadn't even thought to bring me.

My hands fisted. I would tell him, but I needed to make sure I wasn't angry when I did so. I needed to wrap my head around it first, and then I could tell Colton so I wouldn't resent him. It wouldn't be fair to anyone if I did.

Because the crux of it was, I didn't want him back.

I wasn't heartbroken in the way others thought I should be. I was *breaking*. And that was the difference. Because Colton had left me and hadn't wanted me the way I wanted him. I had made a fool of myself for him, and now he was gone. Only he had left a certain little something behind. Though not so little when I thought about the ramifications of everything.

I let out a shaky breath and stood before jumping into the shower. I quickly washed my hair, not caring how long the conditioner was supposed to sit. I just needed to be clean, needed to wash away the evidence of my lack of faith in myself.

My periods had always been irregular. So, when I first missed a cycle, I'd noticed, but it wasn't anything out of the ordinary. Then I'd missed a second, and I knew that something was wrong. And now I knew why.

When I got out of the shower, I pulled my hair up on top of my head, not bothering to dry it. I went into the bedroom, pulled on a pair of cute black jeans, ones that I might not fit soon, and quickly pushed that thought from my mind. Then I pulled on a top and a cute little cardigan and went back to the bathroom. I proceeded to blow-dry my hair and put on makeup. I slid into cute shoes and told myself I would go out for a bite to eat. Go to a new restaurant that had nothing to do with Colton and his restaurateur self. Nothing to do with his friends and their places of business. And I would be okay.

Only I wasn't. And I needed to come to terms with that and get over myself. Instead, I let out a breath, looked at myself in the mirror, and figured I looked perfectly respectable. Maybe more like an exhausted librarian, but it worked.

I shook my head, grabbed my purse, and made my way outside.

I lived within walking distance of a cute area, one with a few restaurants that weren't Colton's or his friends', and a shopping district. It was just getting dark out, perfect for dinnertime, and I told myself this was fine.

I wasn't going to call my family or tell them that I had made a mistake and would now have to live with the consequences. I didn't want to deal with their looks. I didn't want to deal with the pity in their eyes, especially since they were all happy and married, and most were having babies. I was the only single one left, dealing with my own issues.

Yet it seemed I'd be starting a family my way. Not how I'd wanted or how I wanted my family to see me, but I would push that from my thoughts.

I raised my chin and told myself I just needed to pretend that I was normal. Act as if I were fine and handling it. And maybe I *would* handle it.

I knew I wasn't acting normally and was headed into dangerous territory, risking making another mistake. Only I was putting one foot in front of the other and making this work. I just needed tonight. I needed to pretend for this bare instant.

The responsible thing would be to go to my sister and have Annabelle hold me as I told her all of my problems. And yet, I had been doing that for far too long—relying on my family when I could handle things on my own.

I could do this. I could do this. I actually couldn't *do this.*

No. I would not let that thought run through my mind again. I was stronger than that. Once the shock wore off, I could make plans and figure things out.

Annabelle had her family now. The twins were adorable and loving and the most precious things in the world. She had her husband, and she didn't need me coming in and disrupting their evening again. I had done that far too many times.

I couldn't go to my big brother Beckett. He and Eliza were married, happy, and had one of Eliza's brothers visiting. They were also preparing their house for foster care and didn't need me interfering with that.

Benjamin and Brenna had a newborn and barely slept as it was. They didn't need my problems. My parents were on vacation, taking a cruise together and enjoying retirement. I wasn't even going to try to get ahold of them.

And then there was Archer and Marc. They were newly married. I had even been a bridesmaid in their wedding. I wasn't going to bother them during their newlywedded bliss.

My family was moving on, and I needed to get with the program.

I kept walking, smiling at others as they walked past. Most people were in pairs, on dates, or just enjoying themselves and friends.

I reached into my bag for my phone and realized I hadn't even brought it. I shook my head, thinking it was no matter. I wanted to scream, do something, and yet I couldn't breathe.

The first drop of rain hit my face, and I looked up, wondering if it was a tear or the sky opening. My thoughts were scattered, and I felt as if I couldn't suck in air, but I kept going anyway. Couples cuddled closer underneath their umbrellas, something I hadn't even bothered to bring. Others went inside restaurants and the little shops. They kept each other dry and safe as they laughed and smiled, kissing one another as they waited for their tables. I kept moving, ignoring the rain as it drenched my newly dried hair and seeped through my clothes and into my skin.

I held back a curse and turned around. I needed to

go home and get dry. Protect my baby. That was what mattered.

"Paige?"

At the deep and familiar voice, I nearly tripped over my feet and skidded into a puddle. I looked up to see Lee, my brother's best friend, as he ran towards me. He'd left a woman in a gorgeous bronze dress standing in front of a restaurant, a frown on her face and an umbrella keeping her safe from the rain. Lee didn't seem to mind that he was getting wet. Instead, he slid his hands through his hair, pushed the damp strands back, and moved forward.

"Paige? What are you doing out in the rain? Come on. Let me get you under the umbrella or something. Shit. You're shaking."

I wasn't cold. I didn't think the shakes would ever come from the cold again.

"I'm fine."

There was something odd about my voice, and I couldn't figure it out. Was this shock? Or just me breaking? After all this time, had I finally truly broken?

Lee met my gaze and cupped my face as he slid his thumbs over my cheeks. "Do you need to go to the hospital? What the hell's going on, Paige?"

"I'm fine." *I wasn't fine.*

He met my gaze again, and my stomach rolled. It had nothing to do with being sick or pregnant. It was

Lee. The guy I'd had a crush on since I was far too young to *have* a crush. Lee seemed as if he had always been there—just so far out of reach that I couldn't hold on to him. He was my brother's best friend, and I wasn't supposed to find him attractive or want more from him. And Lee wasn't the type of guy you wanted more from.

"Lee, darling. We're going to miss our reservations. Just give her the money and go."

I watched Lee's jaw tense as he let out a breath. "I'm taking you home," he whispered before pulling me to his side and trying to shield me from the rain. It didn't matter since we were both drenched at this point, but he still tried. That was Lee, always doing his best, even if the world didn't care.

"Leia, I need to take Paige home. She's my friend."

The other woman, with her gorgeous cheekbones, legs like a giraffe's, and the most beautiful curves I had ever seen in my life, pouted. "But, Lee. You promised."

"I've got to go. I'm sorry."

Leia narrowed her eyes. "Fine. You'll just have to make it up to me." Then she stomped off, taking the umbrella with her.

Lee cursed under his breath. "Well, that was my umbrella."

My gaze tracked the other woman as she turned the corner. "I'm ruining your date. I'm ruining everything."

"Fuck, Paige. What's wrong?"

Everything.

"I need to go home. I left my phone there."

Lee met my gaze and then nodded before taking my hands and walking me around the building to his car. I didn't remember getting in. I didn't remember him taking a blanket out of the back before wrapping it around me and driving me home. Everything was a blur, but I was still present. I had to be.

"Fuck this. If you won't let me take you to the hospital, I'm calling your sister or one of your brothers. Your parents are on a cruise, right?" he asked as he walked me inside my house after taking my keys from my purse.

I shook my head, pulling myself out of my misery. I was stronger than this. I did not break down and act as if I were losing my sanity. I had let the idea of Colten take so much from me, and I would not let him take this, too.

"I'm fine. Really. You don't have to call my family." I let out a shaky breath, then rolled my shoulders back, telling myself I needed to be an adult and deal with this. I walked to my linen closet, pulled out a towel, and then another before tossing one to Lee. "I'm sorry you got drenched because of me. But thank you. I was having a moment out there."

Lee wiped his face but otherwise stood there, dripping on my floor, just blinking. "And that's it? You're not going to tell me what's going on? If you're not going to tell me, then I'm going to call one of your numerous siblings to come over here so you can talk to them. Because you were standing there in the rain alone, Paige. Looking as lost as I've ever seen you. What the hell's going on?" His jaw tensed. "Is it that bastard? Did Colton come back? Do I need to kick his ass?"

He stood there like a stone god, his dark hair slicked back, his beard longer than I had ever seen it, though it wasn't a full one like my cousins tended to have. His dark eyes narrowed, and I wanted to reach out and hold him. Of course, I couldn't. This was Lee, after all. He was a few inches taller than me, and without heels on, I fit under his arm comfortably. Lee was a hugger when it came to those he cared about, and he always gave good hugs.

Sometimes, I never knew what to do with them.

"I just had a moment. Colton isn't here. He's not coming back." My voice didn't break when I said that, and I counted that as progress. "I just had a moment where I needed to think, and then the rain came that I wasn't expecting, and things got out of hand. Thank you for being there. Seriously." I reached out. Gripped his hand. "Thank you for always being there, Lee."

"Paige. Talk to me." He huffed out a breath. "You can always talk to me. I'm not going to judge you. I just need to know. It wouldn't be right for me to leave you right now without someone knowing what happened. So, I'm here. Talk to me."

He would know soon enough. Everyone would. And I'd have to deal with it. I might as well tell someone who wasn't a Montgomery. A man who had never judged me once in my life, even by accident. So, I figured *why not.*

"I'm pregnant."

Lee blinked a few times before sitting down on the stool next to the kitchen island. "Holy shit."

I burst out laughing. I couldn't help it. "Oh, good. We're on the same page with the words that have been running through my mind since I found out. There are a dozen or so tests in the bathroom that all say the same thing. I'm pregnant. Having a baby. With child. All those things that I have no idea what to do with. But it's here. I'm pregnant. It's Colton's. He's gone. And I don't know what I'm going to do. Only, damn it, I'm going to figure it out. Because I'm done being weak. I am done waiting for someone else to help me with the next phase of my life. I'm pregnant. I'm keeping it. And now, I'm going to promptly cry."

And when the tears fell, Lee held me close and didn't say a word. He didn't have to. Because nothing made sense, but it would have to soon. It needed to. I was having a baby. I didn't have time to wallow in my heartbreak any longer.

I would live for me, for my baby, and for no man.

Never again. Because falling in love only hurt in the end, so I wouldn't.

Ever.

CHAPTER 2

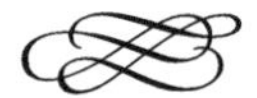

Lee

I'd had dreams all night about a pregnant Paige, angry Montgomerys, and little babies in diapers crawling all around my house. When I woke up, I was confused as hell and wondered why my brain had conjured those images. I finally just pushed it all from my mind and told myself maybe I should stop drinking beer with wheat before going to bed.

Now, I was at work, doing my best to focus on my assignments and not on the fact that one of my good friends was having a baby with a man I wasn't even sure she would be able to speak to again.

I had so many questions, so many thoughts flowing through my head. Paige was one of the strongest people I knew. If anyone could handle this, it was her. And yet I had seen her in the rain. I had seen the look of loss, confusion, and determination sliding over her face as she tried to come to terms with what she had just found out.

And she had told me everything. She hadn't lied or held anything back or said that everything would be fine. Instead, she had bared her secrets to me before she even told her family about the pregnancy. While I wanted to feel pride at the fact that she could trust me, all I could do was wonder how I could help. I had no idea what to do about babies or pregnant women, as my odd dream surmised.

I paused. Maybe that was something I could do. Take the burden off her shoulders. Not that I had the time for that—or the right. We were just friends. She was my best friend's little sister. I didn't get to step in like that. Not that she would let me.

I shook my head, once again focusing on my work.

I was a mechanical engineer and focused on nanotech and robotics. Today, instead of being hands-on with applications and enjoying myself with experiments and testing things out, I was working on a paper. Even in the world of industry and not academics, it was publish or perish. We wanted to get this patent through, so I had to write this paper. And all I wanted to do was cross my eyes and pretend that it was already done. Only here, I wasn't going to get that choice.

My phone buzzed about an hour into figuring out how to condense six months' worth of work into a simple paragraph, and I eagerly set down my book and looked at my phone screen.

Benjamin: *You up for lunch today? I'm near your office and starving.*

I smiled, my stomach growling, and then I remembered that Benjamin didn't know about Paige. It'd only been two days. If she had told her family, I would have heard about it. There would have been the great explosion. Not judgment, not anger, but it would have been something the Montgomerys would have talked to me about. At least, I thought so.

Meaning, if I went to lunch with one of my best friends today, I would have to hide the fact that I did indeed know something they didn't about their baby sister.

Hell. This was why you always stayed away from sisters. It kept things safe that way.

If I didn't text him back or go out to lunch, he would think something was wrong. While I had said no to random lunches with him before because I was busy, I would feel awkward saying no just because I was afraid of keeping someone else's secrets. I shook my head and wrote back.

Me: *Thirty minutes sound good to you? Want to go to our favorite sushi place?*

See. That sounded normal and not as if I were keeping a gigantic secret from one of my best friends.

Benjamin: *Sounds perfect. I could use a spicy crunchy roll.*

Me: *Is it odd that I just want the miso soup? They have the best miso.*

Benjamin: *There's something wrong with you for saying that. While the soup is the best, you're going to get a sushi platter with me. After this long of a day, I need it.*

I tensed, wondering if maybe he knew about Paige and needed to vent. What was I going to say to that? I needed to talk to Paige and get my story straight. Not that I *needed* a story since it wasn't my secret to tell. Why was I making everything so complicated?

Benjamin: *We had a water main burst at the other end of the neighborhood thanks to the city construction, and it screwed up my day.*

Relief flooded me, mostly since Benjamin's stress wasn't about Paige yet. There was something wrong with me.

I signed off with Benjamin and gathered my things, frowning as I saw a note with my name on it at the front desk. "Hey, what's that?"

Andrea, our admin, looked up and pushed the palm-sized envelope towards me. "Not sure. Our courier dropped it off earlier. I was going to head back and give it to you in the next minute or so, but since you're here..." She smiled up at me, her glasses askew in the way that told me her mind was going over a thousand projects right then.

I smiled. "No problem. Thanks, Andrea."

"Are you going out for lunch? Good on you."

I snorted. "Why are you saying it like that?" I pocketed the note and met Andrea's gaze.

She waved me off and fixed her glasses. "Because you never go out to lunch. You work more hours than the boss does. I'm sure they all appreciate it, but I'm glad that you're actually using your lunch for something other than a quick salad at your desk."

"Are you calling me a workaholic?" I asked dryly.

"It's not my fault you called yourself that."

I shook my head, waved, and headed out to the parking lot. It was a nice day, and there wasn't any rain in the forecast, so I figured I could walk the two blocks to the sushi place rather than drive and try to find parking. I pulled the note out of my pocket, the envelope no bigger than my hand, and nearly tripped over my feet as I read it.

I miss you.

The stars are in your eyes.

The moon in mine.

You are mine.

For all eternity.

And for the galaxy's edge.

I frowned, looked over the note front and back, and wondered what the hell I had just read. A nonsensical poem that didn't make any sense?

I frowned, put the note back in the envelope, and then into my pocket. Maybe it was a joke from one of the guys or something. It didn't have a stamp on it, but someone had sent a courier over with it. It also had my name on it, and everything was typed. Maybe it was a friend from school or back in the fraternity being a jerk. We used to like playing pranks on each other when I was younger. Maybe it was one of them.

I didn't know, but when I saw Benjamin getting out of his truck and heading towards the sushi place, I pushed those thoughts from my mind. I had to focus on lunch, my friend, and keeping my secret about Paige out of my mind. I didn't have time to worry about odd poetry that didn't make any sense.

"Hey, you walked over?" Benjamin asked as he held open the door for me. I looked over at the other man, noticed his dark hair and Montgomery-blue eyes. While he looked exactly like his twin, he also had a touch of Paige in him that I hadn't noticed until just now. I wondered why the hell I cared in the moment.

I nodded and held up two fingers at the hostess as we walked inside. She grinned at both of us, her gaze going down Benjamin's body before doing the same to mine. I held back a snort. My best friend was hot, if I did say so myself, but he was happily married and a father to one of the most adorable kids ever.

Of course, that reminded me of Paige, and I quickly thought about something else to say. Anything else. Why was there nothing else to say?

"You're not going to flirt back?" Benjamin asked as we sat down at our usual table, the hostess having left us alone.

I frowned. "No, I'm in the middle of a workday."

"Never stopped you before."

I blinked and looked up at him. "Was I that bad?"

"There's nothing bad about flirting. You're not an asshole. You date, but it's not like you're a cheater or go through women like paper towels or some shit."

I snorted. "That's the analogy you're going to use?"

"I don't know. I'm a married man now. I know nothing about the single life."

I shook my head and leaned into the back of the booth. "Not that you were enjoying yourself around town too much before that."

Benjamin shrugged and toyed with the menu. "I had my moments, but Brenna's all mine now. And I don't need anyone else."

I grinned, thinking about how the two of them had fallen for each other seemingly out of the blue. The four of us, including Beckett, had been friends forever, and yet the two of them seemed as if they'd been made for one another. "I still can't believe you married our Brenna. Dear, dear Brenna."

My friend narrowed his eyes, though they were filled with laughter. "She's my dear, dear Brenna, Lee. Don't you forget it."

I rolled my eyes and smiled at the waiter as he brought us water.

The middle-aged man beamed at us. "Lee, Benjamin, you're back."

I met Benjamin's gaze and snorted. "The fact that you know our names means we might be coming here too much. Is that a bad thing?"

"No, no. I like you two. You're clean, quiet, and easy. I'm calling it a win."

"I'm glad to know that our reputation isn't too bad," Benjamin said with a shrug as he looked over the menu. "You up for the usual?" he asked.

I nodded, suddenly starving. "We'll take the platter M with a side platter A and two miso soups."

"What if I want a salad?" Benjamin asked, folding down the menu.

"Then you would be having an off day since you and Lee seem to love our soup," our waiter said with a laugh as he took our menus back. "I'll get your miso right out, and our chef saw you walk in, so I'm sure they're already out looking for the extra-large platters to fill."

I snorted and shook my head. "I can't help it. I'm a glutton for sushi. And your soup."

"That makes me a happy guy. I'll be right out with the bowls."

He walked off, talking to another table on his way, and Benjamin leaned back into the chair. "Whenever we can bring Beckett, Clay, and/or Archer here, we usually end up taking all of their tuna or something. We kind of wipe out the place."

"It's good food, and I can't help it. I'm a growing boy."

Benjamin rolled his eyes. "Whatever you say. How's work going?"

I took a sip of my water, then leaned back in my chair. "It's going well. I'm working on a paper."

Benjamin winced. "Your favorite thing."

"It's par for the course. Just something I need to do. It's not my favorite thing."

"I would think not."

"It's fine, though. I'm getting through it, and then I can head back into the lab. We just need to work on this patent." I went over my project as Benjamin asked questions, the man's mind brilliant. Then we went back to speaking about Montgomery Builders and their issues for the day.

"It was a main break, then?" I asked as we dug into our soup.

"Yes, some permit or something that didn't go through correctly added on complications. I'm not a hundred percent sure, but I'm not in the mood. We were almost done with this place."

"Is it going to set you back for long?"

Benjamin shook his head. "No, we're making do. I just really needed water to finish planting this tree since it already had a shock to its system. Having water for the whole neighborhood shut off for as long as it was, is annoying as fuck."

"I'd lend you a hand, but we all know that I have a black thumb."

"Very much so, but you are good with the hard labor."

I fluttered my eyelashes. "It is my workout. I have to look pretty."

Benjamin rolled his eyes, and we thanked our waiter as he placed two massive platters of sushi in front of us. I mixed wasabi into my soy sauce, rubbed my hands together, and dug in.

I was full to the brim by the end of lunch, knowing that I would have to work out hard later and probably just eat a salad for dinner. I didn't care. The fact that we could find kick-ass and high-end sushi in Fort Collins, Colorado was a recent turn of events, and I wasn't going to complain.

I went back to work, stayed far too late as usual, and didn't make it home until after dark. My head hurt, but in a good way. I might say I didn't like writing papers or dealing with that part of my job, but I liked working my brain. I also might be decent at manual labor, like Benjamin said, but I preferred the lab, preferred stretching my mind to its capabilities to learn.

I hadn't always had a chance to focus on my studies or who I could be. Not when I was two days out of high school when I became an orphan. Losing both parents so young and barely having the means to take care of myself meant that college wasn't easy. Only I had promised my mom I would go, and that I would try my best. That I'd live my life to the fullest. And since she had been dying in front of me, I hadn't had the heart to say no.

I frowned, wondering why those memories came to the forefront so easily, but I pushed them away and got into my workout gear. I figured a run on the treadmill and then either finishing that movie I had started two nights ago or maybe even reading a paper for work would be something to get me through the evening.

I snorted at that, telling myself I was indeed a workaholic, but I didn't have much else. Most of my friends were all getting married and moving on. They didn't have as much time to go out, which I understood. I worked far too many hours and tended not to have a social life other than the dates I went on. It wasn't like I had a family. Mom had died of cancer when I was eighteen, and my dad... I'd lost him when I was fourteen. But maybe I had lost him years before that. I must have, since he'd done what he did.

A shudder ran through me, and once again, I pushed myself hard on the treadmill, focusing on the paper in my hand rather than the memories I couldn't shake.

I ran for only thirty minutes before my doorbell rang. I frowned and turned off the machine, wiping sweat from my brow as I went to the front entryway. I was chugging water as I opened the door and blinked at the woman in front of me.

"Leia. What are you doing here?"

She smiled at me and pushed her way inside, startling me. I was so taken aback that she was even here since we had only been on a couple of dates, that I didn't stop her when she moved past me.

"I missed seeing you. We had to cut our date short for that woman. And I thought I would see if you'd like to pick things up where we left off."

Considering that things had left off with us not even completing our date, I didn't think her coming to my home unannounced was the answer. However, I wasn't a jerk, so I wouldn't say that.

"You're all sweaty. I like it." She ran her finger down my shoulder, then my arm.

I moved back, out of reach of her touch. "I was working out, and I have some other things to do. I wasn't expecting you, Leia."

"I just wanted to be here. To see you. Don't you want to see me?"

I held back an internal wince, wondering why I had said yes to a date with Leia. Oh, yes, because a friend had set us up. One of my college friends who lived down in Denver had thought of me when Leia asked if he had any single friends. One thing had led to another, and we had gone on two dates.

Two dates, and now she was in my home, unannounced, looking at me with a predator's gaze.

And, honestly, there was no spark between us. I might have had more than a few bed partners in my life, but I needed that spark to want to do anything beyond a few friendly kisses.

I cleared my throat and put a slight smile on my face. "As I said, I have a few things to do, Leia. You're a beautiful woman, sweet, and brilliant. But I'm focusing on work right now, and I just don't think the timing is right."

She stuck out her lip and pouted, and I held back a

wince. "Really? Those are the lines you are going to use? It's not you. It's me?"

"It's not," I lied, wondering what the hell I was supposed to say to get her to leave without sounding like a jerk.

"I just wanted to see you, Lee. I thought we could have a good thing. But are you with that other woman?" she asked.

Annoyance sizzled through me, but I pushed it away. This was my problem, and I had to deal with it. "She's a friend. She needed help. I'm sorry, Leia. I'm just not ready for a serious relationship." And that wasn't a lie.

She studied my face for long enough, I was afraid of what she might say, and how the hell I would get her out of my house. "I see. Well. I guess I'll be around when you change your mind. And you will, Lee because I'm a great catch."

She lifted her chin, and then, before I could think, she pressed her lips to mine. I put my hands on her hips, trying to keep her steady and push her away, but she seemed to take it as an invitation. She wrapped her leg around me, moving closer, and groaned. I pushed her away then, ripping my lips from hers.

"That's enough, Leia. You're nice, and you're going to make somebody very happy. But that's not going to be me."

Her eyes narrowed. "You liked it. I know you did."

"Leia."

She waved her hand in the air. "Fine. Call me when you come to your senses." And with that, she walked out, leaving a trail of perfume and confusion in her wake.

I had no idea who the hell that woman was because it wasn't the same one I had gone on dates with. Was it?

No. It must have been her. That was the problem before. There hadn't been a true connection. Considering that I wasn't a man who wanted a full-time relationship and didn't want to get married or have kids or deal with any links like that, I usually dated women I knew I wouldn't fall for.

That was on me. And now I needed to deal with the consequences.

I went about the rest of my night in a blur, eating a salad over the sink while thinking about work, Leia, and Paige.

I pulled out my phone, checked the time, and knew it wasn't too late to text someone I probably shouldn't be texting.

Me: *Hey, you doing okay?*

Paige: *I'm fine. Okay, I guess. I'm going to tell the family this weekend.*

I swallowed hard and almost called her but thought

better of it. That would require me to actually use my voice, and it would put Paige on the spot.

Me: *That's good. Because I had lunch with Benjamin today, and it was odd to keep it a secret.*

Paige: *Oh, I'm so sorry. I didn't mean to put you in the middle of it.*

Me: *I don't mind. I'm glad I was there for you to lean on. I'll always be there, Paige. You know that.*

Paige: *I do. Honestly, I do. And thank you for being there. I'm going to tell them this weekend, and then I don't know, I'll just figure things out.*

Me: *Do you want me to be there?*

Paige: *Seriously? You'd do that?*

I swallowed hard, wondering why the answer was *yes*.

Me: *It's free food, and it's the Montgomerys. I'm usually always there. But yes, I'll be there. If you want.*

Paige: *I should be able to do this independently, but I want you there. Just so someone else knows, and I don't chicken out. Thank you, Lee.*

Me: *Anything, Paige. Promise.*

I set down my phone, wondering what the hell I was doing. But then again, Paige was the one dealing with the hard things. I could be her friend. Be there. And then I could go back to my normal life. Of work, eating salads in the kitchen, and pretending that I was fine with being who I was.

CHAPTER 3

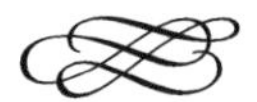

Paige

My family was big, loud, joyous, a little angsty, and full of love and protection.

It didn't matter what mood I was in. I knew there would be someone in the room ready to listen to me, fight with me, alongside me, or to be there to make me laugh. Like I would be there for them.

And yet, right now, I wasn't quite sure what I was ready for or what I wanted to have happen once I told them my news. Everything was going to change as soon as I spoke up. Hell, everything had already altered irrevocably, only they didn't know it yet. My stomach roiled, and I told myself that I was ready for this. That I just needed to rip off the tension like a Band-Aid.

Archer came to my side, a brow raised. "Why are you drinking club soda in the corner, your hand practically shaking? Is something wrong?"

Honestly, while I wasn't surprised it was Archer who had noticed my mood first, it could have been any of my siblings, their spouses, or my parents. They were all observant and inquisitive about one another. I was probably the worst of the lot when it came to knowing what was wrong with my family and wondering how I could help. Others might call me nosy, and they could be correct, and yet, right then, I cursed my intentions.

"Just enjoying my drink."

"Really?" he asked dryly, and I shrugged.

"Really. Is that not okay with you?" I singsonged, and Archer rolled his eyes like I wanted him to.

"You are such a dork, but so am I. It's why we are brother and sister."

"True. Is Marc on the deck with dad?" I asked after a moment.

Archer nodded, a small smile playing on his face. "Yes, Dad is operating the grill. Therefore, Marc is patiently listening and learning."

I held back another smile. "As if Marc doesn't know how to use a grill."

"Dad is just teaching him the finer points of the

Montgomery secrets when it comes to cooking with fire." Archer held up his hands in front of his face, fingers pointed upwards as he lifted his strong jaw and grinned. "It's an art." His blue eyes twinkled, and his dark brown hair, the same color as mine, fell over his face.

I scowled and moved his bangs away from his eyes. "You need a haircut."

Archer shrugged and pushed his hair fully back. "Maybe. I'm trying to see if I can let it grow as long as Riggs'. He has a cute ponytail."

I shook my head, a memory coming to the surface. "You had a ponytail when you were in college, remember? You hated it."

"Because I looked like Paul Revere ready to warn the town that the British were coming. However, I use better products now. I can make a ponytail work. I can look like a hot cover model from one of your books."

"First off, they're your books, too. We read the same romances, brother of mine."

"Touché."

"Second, you'd look cute with long hair. You look good with anything, Archer. It's annoying, actually."

Archer just rolled his eyes. "Says the woman who gets looks whenever she walks around the town in jean shorts and a shirt with holes in it."

I shook my head. "Sometimes, I don't feel like getting adorably cuted-up. It happens."

"Whatever. It's still not fair that your skin is so much brighter than mine."

"It's my youth." I winked, though nausea threatened that had nothing to do with this conversation.

Archer scowled. "You are not very nice."

"What? Just because you are far closer to thirty than I am, doesn't mean that you're aging."

"Ouch," Annabelle teased as she came forward. "What did I say about making fun of Archer's age when I'm around? We are twins, Paige. You may be the baby of the family, and you'll always be younger than us, but that doesn't mean you can call me old." Annabelle laughed as she said it, her newly shorn hair framing her face perfectly.

Annabelle usually had long waves that went down past the middle of her back but had recently cut it in an inverted bob above her shoulders. It looked great on her, and I loved the look. Annabelle said it was easier to maintain with twins at home, and I believed her. I played with my hair, wondering if I should cut mine for when the baby came.

I blanched. The morning sickness that was never just in the morning threatened to come up again.

"Are you okay? I was only teasing. Are you going to be sick?"

I shook my head at Annabelle's words, knowing I needed to get this over with, but now wasn't the right time. Maybe I would do it after dinner or right before. I wasn't sure, but it would have to be soon. I'd for sure do it once everyone had arrived, rather than wait to split it up and do it more than once.

"I'm fine. I'm just a little hungry."

"There's a cheese and vegetable plate on its way," my mother said as she walked into the living room and put the back of her hand on my forehead.

I rolled my eyes. "Mom."

"You're my baby. Of course, I need to make sure that you're not running a fever." Then Mom did the same to Archer, then Annabelle, and the twins laughed.

"You will always be my babies."

"Oh, good. Now I'm going to be singing a Mariah Carey song for the rest of the day," Archer grumbled, but I just laughed.

"Yes, because we all know how much you hate singing Mariah Carey songs. She's your least favorite artist ever."

Archer staggered back. "Okay, that was sacrilege. Don't even joke like that. She was your favorite, too if I recall. Just like we lusted over Blink 182."

I shook my head, grateful that my brother could always make me laugh. "Can I help you get anything else ready for dinner, Mom?" I asked as Annabelle went off to check on the twins. They were sleeping upstairs in the nursery that Mom had built for all of her grandchildren. Brenna and Benjamin's child was sleeping, as well. And today, my parents would know that they would need more space for another baby. Only not for Beckett and Eliza, unless their adoption came through decently soon.

I was doing things out of order, something very unlike me.

Mom smiled and patted her hip. "Everything's going well. You know, at some point, I might just cater this."

"Are you okay, Mom?" Beckett asked as he walked in, handing Mom a glass of wine. "You just said the word *cater*. Are you feeling okay?"

I looked at my mother, studying her face, worried. "Seriously. You've never used that word before."

My mom waved us off. "It was just me rambling. I love cooking for all of you, and I'm never alone in doing it. You guys never let me do everything. You're all so helpful."

"Because we're not going to make you cook for forty people every time we meet up for dinner," I said, shaking my head. "You're going to need to let us take more responsibility if you're even thinking the word *cater.*"

"Maybe. Or perhaps I just want to go and cuddle my grandbabies as soon as they wake up."

As if on cue, Brenna walked in, Rafael cuddled in her arms.

"I'm pretty sure this little one heard his grandma's yearning."

My mom clapped her hands together and moved forward, taking the baby from Brenna's arms. "Hello, darling. Grandma loves you." She hummed and rocked Rafael as Brenna leaned forward and tucked the swaddled infant in tighter.

Benjamin moved to stand behind Brenna, a small smile playing on his face. It always shocked me that my big brother could be so soft with his wife. He had melted into a pile of goo the moment he held his baby for the first time, and I couldn't help but wonder what the family would think when there wasn't a man standing behind me. It would only be me holding the infant, wondering what would happen next.

Of course, that all might change. When I told Colton, something I needed to do as soon as he called me back, he could end up moving back to be a father. I wasn't going to relocate to New York for him. He hadn't asked me when I thought he loved me, and I didn't think I could move for this. Or maybe I should. Maybe it would be best for the baby.

Why was everything so confusing?

"Knock-knock," a familiar and wanted voice said from the other side of the house, and I tried not to let the relief show on my face. Lee walked in, his dark hair brushed back from his face, his jaw cleanly shaven. He'd had a slight beard the last time I saw him, and I blinked at the look of his strong jaw and soft lips.

And that was enough of that. Pregnant women didn't get to have dirty thoughts about their brother's best friend. There were rules about that. Especially when I was about to tell my family that I was pregnant, alone, and losing my damn mind.

"Lee," my mother said as she turned to show off the baby in her arms. "You're here."

"And I was going to steal a baby for some cuddling, but if I have to fight you, I don't think it's going to happen."

Annabelle and Jacob walked in at that moment, an infant in each of their arms, and Lee rubbed his hands together. "Mine, all mine," he teased.

I shook my head, grateful that he was here. Somebody in this room knew my secret. And it didn't feel wrong. Yes, it was a burden, but it wasn't only mine. Maybe it was wrong that I was forcing him to keep my secret for just a few moments longer, but I was glad that I wasn't alone in this.

He plucked my nephew out of Jacob's arms, looked at me, and winked. There was a seriousness in his gaze before he blinked it away, as if he weren't even sure why he had done it.

Or maybe I just saw too much in the looks that Lee gave me. I always had when it came to him. But that was my problem, not his.

"I see you're just in here snatching babies from their parents' arms, acting as if you aren't the fun uncle who will hand them right back as soon as you think you may have to change a diaper."

"I have yet to change a Montgomery diaper, and I don't plan to. Even when we're all old and living in the Montgomery commune, I will hire that out."

"So, you think you're going to be invited to the Montgomery retirement commune?" Benjamin asked, his lips twitching.

"I'm pretty sure I could find a way in." Lee met my gaze for a second, and I had no idea what that was about. Then again, maybe I was just nervous.

"We can have an annex for friends of the family." Annabelle grinned, then looked at her son and daughter. "We need to feed the babies, and then I'm going to be starving."

"I'm already ravenous," Brenna said as she moved to the couch and adjusted herself to begin feeding Rafael.

Annabelle sat on the couch as Jacob pulled out a nursing pillow and helped adjust my niece to start her dinner. Then Lee moved forward, and Jacob scowled. "Excuse me. I will be doing this."

"Yes, because I intended to come here and check out

your wife's breasts as she fed your kids. Stop with the being territorial." Lee rolled his eyes but handed my nephew to Jacob. Jacob's lips twitched and then he adjusted my nephew on the other side of the pillow so Annabelle could feed two at once.

My hand went to my stomach of its own volition, and I let out a breath.

What if I were having twins? I would be outnumbered. If Colton didn't come back, if he decided that this was too much, I would truly be out of my depth. Who would hold the pillow for me and ensure that I could handle feeding both twins at once? I would have to take turns, leaving one baby hungry and crying for me as I fed their brother or sister.

Archer moved forward and cupped my elbow. "What's wrong, Paige?"

I looked at all of them, at my father and Marc as they walked in, and knew I needed to do it now. Just had to get it out there, so it wasn't hiding beneath the surface, waiting to be screamed later. I didn't want to keep secrets. Not with the family I loved with all my heart.

I had wanted to tell Colton first, but he hadn't called me back. I had called twice and was now afraid that he was thinking that his ex-girlfriend was clingy and wanting too much. I would like to think that he was too busy to call me back. But something was off.

He didn't want to talk to me. Had moved on with his new life. That should be fine, but he had left part of his old life unfinished, and I didn't want to send an email or leave a voicemail saying that he was going to be a father.

Or at least, that I was going to be a mother.

Lee came to my side, a brow raised, and I swallowed hard. I wanted to grip his hand for strength, but I knew that would likely send the wrong message. Instead, I stood as near to him as I could without touching. I looked at my family, all of them, and swallowed hard.

"I have an announcement," I said, as everyone turned to me, their gazes intent.

"What's wrong, honey?" Mom asked as she leaned into Dad, and I let out a breath.

"I wanted to tell you all at once, so I don't have to do it multiple times. I'm pregnant." I put my hand over my belly, the words slicing out into the quiet like a hot knife into butter.

Lee leaned closer to me, pressing his body into mine for a bare instant before moving away. It was so quick that I didn't think anyone had noticed, but given the way Benjamin's eyes narrowed, maybe he *had* seen it. I couldn't focus on that, though. Not when my brain was vibrating.

"Pregnant?" my mother asked, the burping towel in her hand falling to the floor. "How? I mean, I know *how*,

Paige." Her voice broke, her hand moving to her lips as her eyes watered.

I hadn't even realized I was crying until I tasted the salt on my lips. "It's Colton's. He doesn't know yet because I can't get ahold of him."

"That motherfucker," Beckett growled.

Eliza gripped his arm. "Beckett, let her finish." My sister-in-law gave me a small smile but didn't reach for me.

I was grateful for that. Everyone stood in place as if waiting for the dam to break, and I wasn't sure what else to do or say to make it any less awkward.

"I just found out. I don't know what I'm going to do, other than I'm having this baby. I know there are a thousand steps and details in front of me, and I'll get there, only I need a moment to take it all in. However, I need to tell Colton first. Then I can make some decisions. I just wanted to let you know and not wait or keep secrets for too long. I'm sorry."

Lee cursed under his breath. "Don't be fucking sorry," he whispered.

"You knew?" Archer asked and then shook his head. "Sorry. It doesn't even matter if he knew first. I'm glad that you had a friend for this." And then Archer held me close, so tight I could barely breathe, and everyone was asking so many questions at once that I couldn't even tell who was speaking.

"Colton hasn't called you back?"

"How far along are you?"

"Are you feeling sick?"

"Have you seen the doctor?"

"I'm going to fucking castrate Colton. I promised I would once, and I'll do it."

I looked up at Annabelle at her words, a watery laugh escaping my lips. "No castration."

"Is castration a thing in your family?" Lee asked as he leaned in, his lips pressed against my ear.

"Not really. Although it might be now," I teased, grateful for his presence. Because he was making me laugh and smile, and all I wanted to do was run. I felt like my family was so disappointed in me, even though it didn't look like it on their faces. They were worried for me, and yet it felt as if I were doing something wrong. That I had broken their trust or made a mistake. I didn't know. I knew this was possibly all in my mind, but I just needed to focus and get through the next few moments without breaking down.

I looked at them all and swallowed hard. "I'm pregnant. I don't know what I'm doing. And I need to go."

And before they could say anything, I turned on my heel and ran, tugging out of Lee's grip as he tried to pull me back. I was already at my car by the time Annabelle caught up to me.

"I just... I need a minute."

"We love you."

My heart hurt so much it was hard for me to keep standing. "I know you do, Annabelle. I know."

"We all love you. They would all be out here with me, but we didn't want to overwhelm you, and I sort of pushed my way to the front. Although Lee almost tackled me. I'm pretty sure it was only because I handed him a baby that he didn't pull me away completely."

There was a questioning look in her gaze, and I shook my head. "Lee was just there when I needed to break." I told her about the rain, of finding out, and then Annabelle held me and kissed my temple. "We love you, Paige. We've got this."

"You don't need to have this," I said as I pulled away. "You have your families—all of you do. I don't have anyone. I thought I had Colton once, and I was wrong. So wrong. I was so naïve. I don't have anyone but this baby now, and it doesn't even feel real yet. But here I am. I'm going to figure this out. And I don't want the family to think that this is their burden or that they have to put down everything to help me. I'm not a baby anymore. You all have these wonderful families around you that you need to focus on. I can do this, Annabelle. I promise." I didn't know if I was lying, but I knew I needed to be alone for the time being so I could find the strength to be the person my baby needed.

I squeezed Annabelle's hand and then moved away,

and she let me. Her eyes were wide, and I couldn't read her face. I used to always be able to read the emotions on her face.

But no longer.

And so, I got in my car, turned on the engine, and left, knowing that I needed to do this on my own.

I needed to do one thing independently and not rely on my family as I did for everything else.

At least, I needed to try.

CHAPTER 4

Lee

"Lee?" Beckett spoke from my side, and I turned to him, running my hands through my hair.

"Hey there."

"Is Paige okay?" My friend's words were soft, hesitant, and it surprised me that he was asking *me* about Paige. Then again, they'd all just been thrown for a loop, and I at least had a couple of days' notice to get my head on straight.

In all honesty, I had expected Beckett or Benjamin to get angry at me for knowing about what had happened with Paige and not telling them. Yes, keeping

Paige's secret had been my only choice, but it was also the only one I would have made. Yet these guys were my best friends. In another time, I would have told them that their sister was in trouble. Only it wasn't my place to say anything. Now, my mind was running in circles.

"I mean…I think so. She's strong. I don't know," I said after a moment, my words honest. Benjamin came to stand next to Beckett, another frown on his face.

"Did you know when we had lunch?" he asked, and I sighed.

"Yes. I did." Since Annabelle had already given me a look when she walked inside, I had a feeling she knew the whole story of why and how I knew, so I might as well tell the guys. "I caught her outside when we had that rainstorm, and she was acting weird. Walking without a coat or an umbrella. So, I made sure she got home safely and was warm. And because I threatened to rat out her behavior as odd to one of you, she told me what was going on. Or at least what she had just found out." I shrugged, my hands in my pockets as I tried to ignore how they stared at me. They weren't glaring or acting as if I had done something wrong, so I counted that as a win.

"Damn it," Benjamin muttered under his breath. "I'm glad you were there. Hell, Paige is usually so level-headed, even when she gets excited about something. She's the one we rely on when things get insane."

Beckett began to pace. "Exactly. Do you know what I want to do? I want to fly to New York and beat the shit out of Colton."

I fisted my hands once I let them out of my pockets and let out a calming breath. "Honestly, that's what I want to do, too, but Colton doesn't know what's going on yet."

Beckett frowned. "Then we'll tell him as we're beating his face in."

I shook my head. "She won't appreciate that. And you know it."

"But it would help me. And, honestly, that's all that matters," Beckett grumbled, clearly lying. "I wanted to hurt him for leaving her as he did. For making all of us think that he wanted more and acting as if he were ready to join our family, and then walking away as if he didn't have a fucking care in the world."

"I'm right there with you," I snarled. "That motherfucker thought that he could just hurt Paige like that? No, the only reason I didn't speak to him myself was that Paige wouldn't have appreciated it." Benjamin met my gaze, and I shrugged. "She wouldn't have. And you know it."

"You're right, but it doesn't mean I have to like it.

What are we going to do when Colton finds out and reacts poorly?" Benjamin asked.

I shook my head. "I want to say it's none of our business, but from the looks on your faces, I don't think that's the case."

It was Eliza who spoke up as she walked towards us. "It *is* none of our business until Paige wants it to be so. And then I will help Annabelle castrate him."

"Oh, so we're doing the castration thing. I'm in," Brenna stated as she clapped her hands together.

I met the other men's gazes and took a safe step back. "You're all way too scary."

"Of course, we are. Our family has been threatened. How dare Paige be left hurting like this?" Eliza raised her chin. "Paige was there for me when I needed her, so I'm going to be there for her."

"She walked away, though," Annabelle said after a moment. "She said that she wanted to handle this on her own because she didn't want to bother us with her issues." Annabelle let out a breath and looked around the living room as everyone talked amongst themselves about plans for Paige and what they thought she'd *let* them do.

"I'm going to head out," I said after a moment.

"Are you going to check on Paige?" Annabelle asked.

I frowned. "I don't know. I need a minute to think. I hate that Paige is hurting, but there's seemingly nothing we can do. First, she needs to do a few things on her own. You know? To figure out what she wants. But she knows you will all be there for her. Hell, so will I. She's Paige."

"She's Paige," Benjamin whispered, meeting my gaze again. I said goodbye to the others, cuddled the babies one last time, and made my way out of the house. I didn't even realize I was heading towards Paige's place until I pulled into her driveway, calling myself a fool.

Paige wouldn't appreciate this. She had left the dinner so she could be alone and think and not rely on the Montgomerys. But then again, I wasn't a Montgomery. I was just a friend. Maybe that's what Paige needed.

I got out of the car, made my way to the front door, and hoped to hell she didn't push me away. Paige answered quickly, a scowl on her face before her eyes went wide. "I thought you'd be one of my brothers. What are you doing here?"

I studied her face, the red-rimmed eyes, and the fact that she'd piled her hair on the top of her head probably as soon as she walked into the house. She wore no shoes and had changed out of her pretty sundress into sweats.

"I know you, Paige." I hadn't meant to say the words, and she frowned at me. She took a step back, and I wasn't even sure she was aware she had done it, but I took it as an invitation, moving into the living room.

She closed the door behind me and turned. "You know me?"

I nodded. "I know how you are with the rest of the Montgomerys. How you don't want to rely on them because you feel that you're…what? The baby of the family?"

She folded her arms over her chest. "I don't know if I appreciate you reading into my intentions."

"Paige, I've known you forever."

"And I've known *you* forever. What does that have to do with this?"

"Because I get it. But in case you haven't noticed, I'm the only single guy in our group. Even Clay and Riggs are married. Everybody is pairing off, starting families. And we're not."

I winced, not having meant to be so blunt.

Paige just snorted. "True. Of course, I *am* starting a family, I guess. In my own way."

My gaze immediately went to her stomach, and Paige lowered her arms to place her palms over her flat belly.

"I'm having a baby, and I don't know what to do with that. I'm still figuring it out. I don't need pity."

"I'm not giving you pity. I'm here to be your friend. Hell, Paige. Like I was saying, everybody else is paired off, finding the next phases of their lives. And, frankly, I'm content where I'm at. I like my job. I like my life. I'm not looking for marriage or futures or anything like the rest of your family."

"Okay." She stared at me, probably wondering where the hell I was going with this. That would make two of us.

"I know this isn't how you planned for anything. I know you like planning and putting things in the right order. I get it, too. I'm not going to say it's going to be easy, but I'll be here. I'll help you through this."

I wasn't even aware I was saying the words until they were out.

"Excuse me?" she whispered. "You're going to be here for me. In what capacity?"

I began to pace, running my hands through my hair. "I don't know. What do you need? Is ice cream something you'll need? Holding your hand when things get tough? You said yourself that the rest of your family is moving on and creating lives. I get that. Hell, I'm happy for them. But I saw how you were afraid of what they might say because you're going about this in a way that none of us ever planned. I don't want you to have to do this alone."

"Again, so, you're going to what? Step up and be here for me? Doing what? Getting me ice cream, holding my hand as you said? Or holding my hair back when I throw up?"

I smiled, thinking back to when we were younger. "I've done that before."

Her cheeks pinked, and I wanted to reach out and feel if they were warm. "When I was drunk."

I shook my head. "Whiskey isn't your thing."

"That was spiced rum that time." Her scowl was so cute. It always had been.

"Okay, so I'm wrong."

"Lee." Paige scowled again.

"I'm not wrong about this. I'm here."

"I don't need your pity," she whispered, repeating her words.

I moved forward and finally let myself cup her cheek. "Then what *do* you need?" My voice was low. I wasn't sure what I needed her to say. Instead, I wiped away her tears and pulled her to my chest. She cried in my arms, her body shaking, and I kissed the top of her head, running my hand down her back.

"I don't know why I'm crying. I'm not upset. I'm just overwhelmed. I don't want my family to be disappointed in me."

I frowned and moved back slightly, my hands still on her. "Why would they be disappointed in you? You're an adult. You're making choices and decisions that affect your life, but you're rational about it."

"I was the one who wanted a wedding and babies and the perfect life with a white picket fence. I was so sure that Colton was going to ask me to marry him." She laughed, but there was no humor in her voice. "I told everybody that he was going to propose. That I was just one step away from joining them in holy matrimony. Whenever Annabelle, Eliza, or Brenna mentioned their wedding colors or who would be a bridesmaid, I always brought myself into it. I talked about the colors I wanted for my wedding. Or how it would be wonderful when we could all rotate who could be the maid of honor or the matron of honor in each other's weddings, so nobody was left out. And yet, it didn't happen for me. And I thought I would be okay. But now…this. I set myself up for this amazing thing, and when it failed, I saw the looks on their faces. They don't blame me, but they feel sorry for me. And it's only going to get worse. The single mom whose boyfriend didn't want her."

I cursed under my breath. "Paige."

"I don't want to feel sorry for myself, either. It gets me nowhere. Before, I pushed those thoughts out of my mind and pretended that I was okay. And now, things are changing again, and I don't know what I'm supposed to do."

I moved forward and ran my thumb along her jaw. "Paige," I whispered.

She was right there, a bare breath from me. I saw how her blue eyes widened, her mouth parted, and I didn't even realize that I was lowering my mouth to hers until she gasped against my lips. My tongue brushed against hers, and I held back a groan, tasting her salty tears and the sweetness of the creamer from her tea earlier.

I pulled away, my eyes wide, and couldn't believe I had just kissed Paige Montgomery.

My pregnant friend, the same woman who was also my best friend's little sister.

There were so many reasons I shouldn't have kissed her, and yet, it was all I could do not to want more. To relish the taste that would never be mine again.

"What was that?" she gasped as she moved away, her fingers delicately brushing her lips as if she weren't sure if what had happened was real.

That had been the absolute worst thing to do, so I would lie. Lie so fucking well, she would never know.

"I just wanted to get you out of your funk. To remind you that I'm going to be here. A promise. It's just me. Lee. Your friend. Nothing more."

All a lie. Because it was what I was good at—lying to myself when it came to Paige.

She met my gaze, studying my face before nodding, and I had to tell myself that she was doing this to protect herself and her baby, not that it was so easy to brush me off. It shouldn't matter anyway because I *was* going to be her friend. That was the whole reason I was here. There didn't need to be any blurred lines or confusion when it came to the two of us.

"Okay. That's an odd way to get me to stop crying, but it worked." She shook her arms out and then wiped her face. "I need to be a big girl and just do this. I need to stop crying at everything that gets overwhelming."

"I guess I need to be a big girl, too," I said with a laugh, and she snorted.

"So, you're going to do this? Be the person I can talk through all of this with? It could get gross."

I winced. "Thanks. But, seriously, I'm here. Anything you need. Though you know that your family would be there for you, too."

I whispered the last part, and she let out a breath.

"I know. But I also don't want them to worry about me. So, I'll take you up on your offer. At least until I go insane, and you get annoyed with me."

"You don't annoy me, Paige."

"Oh, that sounded like a dare."

I shook my head. "What about Colton?" I needed to ask, had to throw that rock into the calming pond between us.

She winced. "I'm going to call him. Again."

"Why don't you do it right now? Maybe me being

here will be the good luck you need and he'll finally fucking answer."

"You're angry."

I raised my brows. "You bet your ass I am. He hasn't called you back yet. What a douche."

"I want to believe that he's just busy. But you're right, what a douche."

I grinned and then leaned to the side to tap her phone that lay on the kitchen island. "Call him. I'll be here."

She met my gaze and nodded. "Okay. Because you're here."

When she reached for the cell, I tried not to take her words to heart because we were just friends. Nothing more, nothing less.

And I would pretend that I hadn't just kissed the woman I had been trying not to think about for far too long.

After all, she was so far out of my league. It wasn't even a dream that I could dare to have. I knew what happened when you loved too hard. When things broke.

And how you got left behind when it ended.

CHAPTER 5

Paige

I looked down at my phone and let out a shaky breath. "You're really going to be here while I do this?" I asked, not sure what I wanted the answer to be.

On the one hand, I knew this conversation with Colton wouldn't be easy. In fact, I might scream, cry, do both, or not say a single thing other than the truth. And in the end, I wasn't sure how he would react, or if he would even say anything at all.

The problem with Colton was that he was a nice guy. Not the trademarked version of the guy who put you down while claiming he was a *Nice Guy*. Not the guy who thought he owned me.

He was just kind. And dumb.

But I hadn't minded. So what if he sometimes forgot important things? He was usually there for the people in his life in the end. He remembered birthdays and anniversaries. He always remembered our dates and was never late. He enjoyed being early or on time. It was probably because his father had been in the military, and the idea that being on time was late had been ingrained in him from a young age.

I had thought I loved Colton. And perhaps I had. But he hadn't loved me in the way I needed. And when he left, I vowed that I would never need another man again. And yet, here I was, asking Lee if he would stay while I told the father of my child that he was going to be a daddy.

I frowned as Lee studied my face. He shrugged and then leaned back. "I'm going to be here because I said I would help you out. I won't say a word unless you need me to. I can even do my best to draw a picture of him so you can throw darts at it."

I snorted, liking the idea of finding a way to use my rage. "Or you could just print out a photo."

"That requires a photo printer and wasting a lot of ink. I can just hand draw a lovely photo of him."

"I didn't even realize you could draw."

"I don't have an inch of talent. However, I *can* draw a decent stick figure. I'm sure I could make a stick figure of him for you."

I burst out laughing, surprised that I could even laugh at a time like this. There was just something about Lee. He made me all warm inside and happy. He made me laugh. He had always done that. From the first time my brothers brought him home to meet us, Lee had been there, making us smile and play around.

Lee was quiet about his past and his family. He was great at letting others lean on him if we needed it, but he rarely shared where he came from, other than being my brothers' friend. I knew he was from Colorado, though he'd moved around some as a kid. And he was a player. He was also brilliant—his mind fascinated me.

I had been decent at math and science in school, only because I enjoyed patterns. But once you had to layer on the concept of researching and diving into the unknown with your hypotheses, I wasn't there for that type of math and science. And yet, that's who Lee was. He always asked questions and fought to find answers. That was what drove him. At least, what I could see from the outside.

He was so different from Colton.

I had to wonder exactly why I was comparing the two at this moment. I shook my head and rolled my shoulders back, preparing to do what I must. It was inevitable. "I'm not going to throw darts at a stick version of him or the nicely done photo. Don't worry. This is going to go great. I'm totally not going to panic and break down."

"I'm not sure if I enjoy the sarcasm in your tone. It's not like I can give you a drink to calm you down."

"Thank you for reminding me that I can't have alcohol for another nine…eight months? Or, wait, I can't have alcohol if I'm breastfeeding, either. I mean, if what I remember reading during Annabelle's and Brenna's pregnancies was right. Or maybe TV and movies have led me wrong this entire time. That means if I decide to breastfeed, something I haven't even decided on fully yet because God forbid I'm able to process what's going on, I'm probably never going to be able to have alcohol again. I had my last drink—a hard seltzer, by the way, and it was horrible—and I didn't even know it."

"Please tell me you didn't drink a White Claw," he whispered.

"I was out of everything else, and a friend who brought it to drink left it at my house. It was either that or whiskey straight at six in the evening on a Tuesday. I should have had the whiskey."

"I feel like I need a whiskey now."

I narrowed my eyes. "If you drink in front of me, we're done. You're just going to have to walk right out."

He grinned. "I promise I'm not going to drink in front of you. That would be wrong. Very wrong. For now."

"Jerk." I laughed.

"I know. However, you are laughing. So, I'm counting that as a win."

I sobered instantly, as did he, and I pulled my phone closer. "Here we go." I pressed Colton's name and frowned. "He's probably not even going to answer. He hasn't before. All this wind-up for me having to send him a telegram."

"Please make it a singing telegram if he doesn't answer," Lee whispered.

I met his gaze and pressed my lips together so I wouldn't laugh.

"Oh my God. I will help you write the song to explain it. And we can do it in public. Because if he doesn't fucking answer, he deserves it. Oh, great, there could be dancing." Lee practically rubbed his hands together, and I shook my head, my lips twitching.

"Paige?" Colton's voice came through the line as I put it on speakerphone, and I shook, looking up at Lee. My mouth opened, but no words came out.

"Paige, is that you? I had to get a new phone. I dropped mine at work and didn't get to the store until yesterday. But hell, so good to hear from you. However, I do not hear you. You there, babe?"

I cleared my throat as Lee mouthed the word *babe,* a single brow raised in question.

I shook my head, feeling odd at the sound of Colton's voice. There was nothing there. No twinge, no yearning. Had I only been in love with the *idea* of love and getting married and moving on with my life?

Because if I felt nothing after what? Two months or so after seeing Colton last, then what the hell was wrong with me?

"Hey. I'm sorry to hear about your phone. That makes sense why you didn't call me back."

"I'm sorry, babe. I didn't mean not to call you. I'm not that much of an asshole. But hell, I'm so glad you called."

I cringed. "I sure hope you're still happy once I finish what I have to say."

Colton didn't seem to hear me, however. "I wanted to tell you something in person, but hell, let's do it right now."

I frowned, confused as Lee gave me an odd look. I shrugged, and he winced.

"Paige, babe, I know it's fast, but we both said that we wanted to be friends when we ended things. So, I have to tell you this."

I hadn't said anything of the sort. I'd been so confused about him walking away. Lee just frowned, his jaw going tense.

"Babe, I found someone. Like, really found someone. You would love her. It was like love at fucking first sight, Paige."

The ground fell out from under me as if jagged rocks were torn from the hardwood beneath my bare feet. I looked down at my phone, wondering what circle of hell this was in *Dante's Inferno*. It wasn't jealousy. It wasn't lust. Perhaps it was rage. Or a new special circle of hell for me. One where I watched a man I had thought I loved, one who hadn't wanted to settle down yet and then moved across the country to get away from me, find the love of his life and be *so* glad to tell me.

"What?" I asked, my voice strained.

Lee moved forward, a scowl on his face, and I held up my hand, palm out, telling him to stop. He didn't say anything, and for that, I was grateful, because I had no idea what the hell I was supposed to say, let alone let Lee say anything in that moment.

This wasn't exactly how I'd expected this call to go.

"Seriously, though, Paige, you would love her. She's beautiful, brilliant. She's just so good at what she does. She's a restaurateur out here and just amazing. Paige, babe, I proposed. I know it's too soon, only like two months, but when you know, you know, right?"

My mouth dropped open, and I met Lee's gaze. I wanted to laugh. There was no crying. I needed to laugh and pretend that this joke would just be over. But Lee simply looked at me, his face telling me that he was just as confused as I was.

"What the fuck?" Lee whispered, and I waved him off, not wanting Colton to hear him.

"Are you there, Paige? I'm getting fucking married. You would love her. I cannot wait for you to meet her."

"Colton?" I asked, my voice shaky.

Colton kept going on and on about this woman named Tarryn, and well, she did sound like a wonderful woman. And maybe I *would* enjoy meeting her. We could have been best friends. I could be her maid of honor at her wedding to my ex-boyfriend. Everything would be great, and she'd be beautiful and happy and have the life that I thought I wanted. But hell no. What the hell was happening? It didn't make any sense. No sense at all. And I could only stand there and listen to Colton go on and on about this woman, when all I wanted to do was scream and tell him that no...that wasn't going to happen. I couldn't let it, damn it.

Maybe it would be a secret baby in one of those romance novels that I loved, but that was always my most hated trope. I despised it because it made no sense. Why would a woman keep that secret? And yet, standing here and listening to Colton go on and on about a woman he just met that he would marry and how he didn't understand why this could possibly break me, I knew I had to tell him the truth. It was so fucking stupid. This was the father of my child. This was the DNA this baby would share.

I would not let my baby grow up to be as stupid as Colton.

"Colton? I'm pregnant."

Lee looked at me, then threw his hands up into the air and began to pace. I wished I could do that just then, but I was afraid I would throw up if I moved. And that vomit would have nothing to do with morning sickness.

"Babe, you found someone? I'm so fucking happy for you."

I rubbed my temple as Lee pretended to strangle Colton using his hands in the empty air, and I gritted my teeth. "No. You asshole. You stupid, stupid asshole. It's yours. And, apparently, you are moving on nicely, and I'm still here, picking up the pieces. We're going to have a baby. We're going to have to figure something out. And while I would love to keep this secret, I can't. So, congratulations on the engagement. Oh, and you're going to be a father."

"Oh my God. Are you sure?"

I wanted to toss the phone across the room. How much of an idiot was I that I had loved this man? Was this my taste? Dumbasses who couldn't understand what the words coming out of my mouth meant? Was my taste so horrible that I had put myself in this situation because I was an idiot? Maybe I was dumb. Perhaps I didn't get the science and math that Lee had gotten because I was a fucking idiot. Maybe my family only gave me my job at Montgomery Builders because they felt sorry for me. They didn't need me to organize their lives or plan everything when it came to a multi-million-dollar company. No, they could do that on their own with an online scheduler. They didn't need Paige Montgomery because I was a fucking idiot who always fell for the wrong fucking men.

"Are you sure?" he asked again, and I nearly threw the phone.

"I know I'm pregnant, Colton. I have taken multiple tests, including one from a doctor. I can send them all to you if you want. But yes, I'm pregnant."

There was a long pause, and I nearly screamed.

"And it's mine? Are you sure?"

"Are you kidding me right now? You're serious. You're actually seriously asking me that question."

Before I could say anything else, Lee grabbed the phone before Colton could repeat his question or dig the hole any deeper. "Get your head out of your ass and figure out what's going on, and she'll call you back. But don't you dare question her like that again."

"Oh, Lee," Colton said. "I'm so glad you're there. You're good for her. She needs a friend."

Lee just blinked at me and then hung up the phone. He set it down on the counter and then ran his hands through his hair.

"Oh my God," I whispered.

"Seriously," he growled.

"I can't... What just happened? How did he...? How was I so stupid to be with someone that stupid? Was he always that dumb? Why didn't you guys tell me?"

Lee just blinked at me as if coming out of a trance. Something I truly wanted to do, as well. "Paige. He's like a fucking puppy. He didn't even think I was the one who was fucking you. He thought I was just your friend. First, he thought you were fucking someone else. Then he questioned if the baby was his. And as soon as he heard my voice, he immediately assumed I was your friend. He didn't think the baby was mine. He just presumed that we were just so sweet and happy that I would clean up his fucking mess. Not that this is a mess, because I'm not calling your baby one, but dear God, what an idiot."

I looked at him then, my mind a little slow as I pieced that together. "That's what you're worried about?"

"Not fully, but hell. He thought the baby wasn't his for a minute, and then as soon as I got on the phone, he immediately assumed I was your friend. I just don't get it. What the hell is in between that guy's ears?"

"I don't know. What the hell is happening? What did I see in him?"

I began to pace, then Lee took my hand and pulled me to him. "I don't know what you saw in him, but it seems he's happy enough moving on, even though this sort of threw a big wrench. But hell, Paige. You don't need him. You can do this on your own." The manic look in his eyes surprised me, but I didn't say anything. I wasn't sure I *could* say anything.

"I don't know what to do," I whispered.

"I'm here, Paige. Let me help." He looked as surprised by the words as I did.

"What?" I whispered.

"I don't know, Paige. But you know your family is too much right now. Even if they mean well and are my best friends, you walked away from that house because it was too much for you at that moment. And I get it. I get that watching them live their lives with everything going on and how wonderful they are can be a lot. I've got work. That's it. So, let me help. You clearly can't talk to Colton about this." He ran his hands through his hair and began to pace once more.

"Are you serious right now?"

"I am. Let me help. I'll be your labor partner or whatever they call it. When I'm not working, I'll be here for you. We both know that your family is busy. And that you have this weird thing when it comes to them."

"Weird," I growled, hating that he saw me so well.

"It's true. So, let me help. I have no idea why I'm offering, other than we're friends. And Colton pisses me off. Let me be here."

I looked at him then, wondering if I had been the one to lose my mind much like Colton had, and if Lee was doing the same.

"You know what? Why the fuck not? I'm already doing things out of any semblance of order. Why not have my brother's best friend help me as my labor coach?"

"Good. We can figure out exactly what the hell that means later."

I looked at him and burst out laughing before he wrapped his arms around me, and I hugged him tightly. There were no tears. This farce that was my life couldn't get any stranger. Why not lean on Lee?

At least, for the moment.

I could ignore the twinge inside that I had thought long buried.

It'd be good for everybody if I never thought about that twinge again.

CHAPTER 6

Paige

I paced around my house, dictating things I needed to get done for the day into my notes. I'd had a long morning dealing with Montgomery Builders' issues, but I thrived in it. I loved working with my family and finding answers to problems that others couldn't. While I might've teetered on the edge of a nervous breakdown, wondering if I fit in with my family and if I was too stupid because of my taste in men, I knew my worth. I had just needed a moment to breathe and to wonder why Colton was the way he was.

I had only heard from him once in the past few days, saying that he didn't know what to say and needed time to think. That was fine with me. I needed time to consider things, as well. I had another doctor's appointment coming up soon, and then, after that, maybe I'd have answers for myself, as well as answers from Colton. It still surprised me that Lee, of all people, had been the one to say he'd help me. And while I had agreed to it, I didn't think Lee had fully thought about the offer. It was in the moment. Lee was there for me to have someone to lean on since everything seemed to have gotten a little gray around the edges—especially when it came to my feelings.

Everything felt weird. As if I were reaching the end of an abyss that wasn't truly there. Things were up when they should be down, sideways when they should be right-side up. I wasn't quite sure what I was doing, but work could settle me. I needed to focus on getting a few things out of the way for an upcoming project so I could possibly make plans for being a mother. Strategies were helpful. I had watched my sister and sister-in-law work through their pregnancies, and while I had been a bystander and bounced from room to room during the labors, I was going to do this on my own, and I would find a way.

I wouldn't put all of my worry on my family's shoulders. Nor would I let myself lean too hard on Lee. That would lead to too many issues.

My doorbell rang, and I quickly shut off my notes app, annoyed with myself for once again splitting my focus when it came to working. It was a Friday evening, and at one point, I might've been out at Riggs', partying with my siblings. Tonight, I was at home, planning to indulge in junk food for dinner since I didn't have groceries—something that never happened when it came to me, but I'd be distracted. My family wasn't going to be at Riggs' either, for that matter. They all had their spouses and families at home tonight. Evenings at Riggs' seemed like a far-off memory at this point, and now that I was more than likely going to remain a single mother until the end of time, something that scared me and yet thrilled me simultaneously, I probably wasn't going to go to Riggs' again. Unless Riggs somehow let babies come into his bar.

I opened the door and frowned as I looked up at Lee. I blinked, studying his face. "Lee?"

"Hey there." He leaned forward, kissed my cheek, and moved past me into my house. I closed the door behind him, ignoring the tingling feeling on my cheek from where his lips had pressed against my skin. That was enough of that thought. When I looked down at my sweat capris, my two tank tops, and my lack of bra, I wished I'd at least put on a sweatshirt. I was a damn hot mess, but I always seemed to be around Lee these days.

I looked down at my boobs and cursed. My nipples were hard, and it had nothing to do with the aching that came with pregnancy, and everything to do with a certain man in my vicinity. I'd always had that problem when it came to Lee, and I figured it was just a natural reaction. He was hot, single. As was I. Yet neither of us was available for that—especially not together.

I looked down at my treacherous nipples and then back up at Lee as I realized that he was staring at me, his gaze on my face, not on my breasts. See? He didn't want me like that. He wasn't even looking at my nipples.

And I really needed to stop thinking the word *nipples*.

"Why are you here? What did you bring?" I asked him and wondered why my voice was so high. "Sorry, that was rude. Hi, Lee. I didn't know you were coming over. And you brought something? That's nice, but you didn't need to."

"Hi, I told you I'd be by."

"I thought you meant like in passing or eventually. I didn't think you meant tonight." I ran a hand through my hair, grateful that I had showered when I got home so I wasn't a greasy mess. Still, though. "Sorry, I was working."

"*I'm* sorry. Shit. Did I interrupt?"

I looked down at my phone and then set it on the kitchen counter. "No, not really. I was just going through a few notes. Dictating."

"I tried to do that for my job once, and while it understood my voice just fine, the scientific terms, not so much. You'd be surprised by the garbled mess that came out."

I laughed, shaking my head. "Yeah, I could see that being a problem. I have enough issues when I dictate building terms since it tends to censor me if it thinks I'm getting too dirty."

His eyes widened. "Seriously?"

"Seriously. Not that I *am* getting dirty, but you know all the innuendos when it comes to plumbing."

He laughed outright, and I ignored how it lit up his whole face. Hell, were hormones supposed to do this to me already? I was usually pretty good about holding back my desire and want when it came to Lee.

Only right then, it was a little more difficult than usual. I pressed my thighs together, hoping that Lee didn't notice. Damn hormones.

"Anyway, I brought dinner."

I finally looked at the bag that he'd set on the counter and beamed. "Is that Tex-Mex?"

"The best and only Tex-Mex in Fort Collins, Colorado. From a family that moved up from San

Antonio. I'm calling it a win. Eliza's brother, Eli—who's still in town, by the way—said that he would actually eat there, so I counted that as a plus."

"They're Texan. They're picky about their Tex-Mex. Just like we Coloradans are picky about everything else."

Lee shook his head and then began unpacking the bag. "I got fajitas, rice, beans, and a few other things. I figured we could just share everything and see what you think."

"Did you get the carnitas?" I asked while rubbing my hands together.

"Yes, the carnitas, as well as a pepper medley, carne guisada tacos, and carne asada tacos. Did you know the only way I could remember what was guisada and asada is that the G in guisada means gravy for me?"

I shook my head, laughing. "I always mix them up, so now I'm going to remember that."

"Good, well, there's probably too much food, and I don't know what you're keeping down. And, honestly, I wasn't sure if you could do too much spicy food, but most of the jalapeño and srirachas are on the side."

My stomach rumbled then, and I put my hand over my belly, wondering if the baby, however quiet they were for now, would like spicy food.

"I don't know if I should do spicy."

"Everything else is mild. You can add on the spices if

you want. Now, if I were to bring over Indian food, that might be a problem."

"You and I love hot Indian food, but only like medium-hot. The hot-hot just burns off my tongue, and I can't taste any of the actual dishes."

He smiled at me, his dimple peeking out. He was truly too handsome for his own good. He was also too big for my house. Yes, I had a decent-sized two-story home with plenty of room for the baby when it was time to build the nursery, but Lee took up so much space with his mere presence.

Or maybe I saw too much when it came to him, and I needed to rein in my emotions and desires.

"See, this is why we get along. And why we're going to be perfect partners for this. I'm going to make sure that we won't get anything too spicy. However, I *am* craving guacamole."

I pressed my lips together, ignoring how tears threatened. Why was I crying? There was nothing to cry about just then, and yet all I wanted to do was weep in joy that he was here. Screw doing this alone. Lee was just a good person. I could do this. I could lean on him. I would not freak out. And yet, here I was, doing exactly what I said I wouldn't.

Relying on a man. And thinking that I couldn't do this on my own.

"Stop looking like that."

I shook my head at his gruff tone, yet grateful that his words had pulled me out of my spiral. "What?"

"You're going through about a thousand different emotions right now, and I'm not even going to touch on the whole hormonal aspect of things because I don't want you to knee me in the balls."

"Seriously?" I asked, deadpan.

"What? Our friends have been through pregnancies before. Annabelle with twins. Twice the emotions. I know that look. You're asking yourself if you should kick me out right now because you can do this on your own. Because you're a strong, confident woman."

"Now you're just quoting Chandler from *Friends*," I grumbled.

"You know, you weren't even old enough to watch that show when it came out, but thanks to streaming, you can probably quote every single line from the entire ten seasons."

"Of course, I can. Phoebe's the best."

"She is," he teased.

"And, seriously, you're allowed to rely on me. And while you haven't truly questioned why I'm doing this, I'll tell you. Because I like you, Paige. We're friends. I like being your friend. And, hell, I'm so fucking pissed off at Colton right now that I want to fly to New York and beat the shit out of him and make sure he doesn't think that he can just come back here and pretend nothing happened. So, in lieu of doing that, I will be your best friend ever and help you through this. In addition to all that..." he began, raising his chin.

I began to laugh, so confused and yet happy at the same time. Something I didn't think I would feel for a while.

"In addition," he repeated, "I know that your brothers and your sister want to be here right now and take care of you. And if they can't hurt Colton, then they want to make all of your plans for you and make sure that you're never left wanting. I get it. Because that is what they do. That is what you do. You guys are such a tight unit, and I love it. But I also know you want to prove that you can do this on your own. So, you will. And so will I."

I stood there in front of him, feeling as if I were bare to the world as he read me so easily. This was *Lee*. The man I had crushed on and yet hadn't let myself want for more than a moment because he wasn't right for me. I knew he didn't want a future, a family. And yet, here he was, saying he'd help me start mine even in the oddest of senses. The two of us had always been on each other's periphery in our group of friends, connected and yet not. But he'd always been there.

And it seemed as though he'd seen me far easier than I ever thought.

It would be hard to be near him and not wonder

what if, but then again, I'd only wondered when it came to Colton, and look at what I'd become there.

"I'm so utterly confused that you can read me so well. Everything you just said made sense and yet no sense at the same time."

"Welcome to my brain. It is terrifying in here. However, I don't want these tortillas to get cold, and they are the fresh ones. Not store-bought. They made them right there with that little machine that presses them together and cooks them over the open fire. Oh my God, my stomach is growling."

"Are you on some type of drug?" I asked, laughing as I helped him put everything out on plates.

"No, I just don't know how to handle a pregnant Paige. A pregnant Paige who was crying. And, frankly, I've had a shitty day, so I want to laugh and hang out. Okay?"

"I didn't even ask you how your day went," I whispered. "Now I'm the shitty friend."

He leaned down and kissed my cheek. Once again, I ignored the feeling it left behind. "My day was shitty because people suck, and I got like four random hang-ups at work because I think someone has the wrong number and doesn't think it's me and doesn't realize it until they hear my voice."

I stared at him, knowing he was here because I'd told

myself I didn't need my family to help. I was wrong, but at least I was wallowing in my own denial. "That would be annoying. We get a few hang-ups every week at Montgomery Builders. I don't know if it's a prank or a telemarketer asking me about my car's warranty."

"I swear, this is why millennials don't use phones anymore."

"Nope, texting it is. It's only right."

I sat down with him at the bar in my kitchen, both of us facing each other, our knees brushing as we ate carnitas and tacos and fajitas, my stomach all happy with the food. "It's not spicy, and that's good. I don't even know if I should be eating spicy food."

He wiped his mouth, his forearms flexing. "I guess it's going to be in the baby books. Have you started reading them?"

I shrugged, ignoring the panic rising. "I read them for Annabelle and Brenna, but not really from the perspective of the pregnant person. Which, in retrospect, was kind of stupid."

"No, you were reading as the auntie. Now, you get to read as the mom. Pick out the baby book we read first. I'll help."

I just shook my head, wondering why this man was so perfect in this moment. What had I done to deserve him as my friend? "I'm not sure you really want to read a book about pregnancies with me. There's a lot of talk about cervices in there."

Lee didn't even cringe. He just finished up his fajita. "Hey, I can learn. I like learning. That's why I'm a scientist."

There was seriously something wrong with this man. "And learning about the placenta is something that you want to do for fun?"

"I know you're trying to gross me out while we're eating, but it's natural. You're not going to. Believe me. The things I've seen? You're not going to do it."

The way he said it, with a slight brittleness to his tone, I wanted to know what he was talking about, but I didn't ask. Lee was great about joking to push people away, at least on certain subjects. And I, above all, understood. At least, in this situation.

I shook my head, then pulled up my phone as we picked a book to read together. Maybe I was clinging to him because I was nervous about everything else, and I didn't care at that moment. It was nice, and I liked it. And so, I'd pretend. For now.

We cleaned up the dishes, and I leaned against the wall, shaking my head. "I feel gross."

"You're not gross," Lee said as he stood in front of me, so close it scared me. My hormones were on over-drive, and all I wanted to do was lean forward, grip his shirt in my fist, and pull him down to me. Something was seriously wrong with me.

Lee stood in front of me, his lips close to mine, and his eyes darkened.

"Lee?"

"I'm going to do something fucking stupid right now. Don't hit me."

And then he pressed his lips to mine, and I didn't hit him. Instead, I wrapped my arms around his neck and pulled him down even closer. He leaned into me, pushing me against the wall, one hand on my hip, the other above my head, keeping us steady.

"So fucking stupid. What are we doing?"

"I don't know. And I don't want to stop. Okay?" I asked, my voice a whisper.

"I'm still going to help you, Paige. I didn't come over for this."

"We'll blame it on my hormones."

"I don't have those hormones, Paige," he stated before biting my lip. I groaned, arching my hips into him. I felt the hard line of his erection pressing into my belly, that thick cock of his firm, and all I wanted to do was go down to my knees and suck him into my mouth. But I didn't. Because this was stupid. So, so stupid. And yet, it was all I wanted. I just wanted to forget. And when I said as much, his eyes darkened.

"But it's not going to change anything. I just…it can't, Paige." There was no pain, no sadness at his words. Because I didn't want it to change anything, either. I just wanted to pretend, and this was Lee. *This was Lee.*

And then I was kissing him again, and he didn't pull away. This was so idiotic, and we would likely regret it, yet neither of us said anything. It was as if we knew if we spoke, it would make it real, and we'd regret our decision as soon as we finished making it.

He slid his hands up under my shirt and tank top and cupped my bare breast, and we both sucked in a gasp. When his thumb pressed over my nipple, I groaned, and he froze.

"My nipples are sensitive," I whispered.

"Good to know." And then he leaned down, pushed up my shirts, and sucked one into his mouth. I nearly came right then, my panties so wet I knew he'd be able to tell as soon as he touched me. But I didn't care. He kept sucking at my breast, then the other, playing with them both before he went down to his knees and tugged off my sweats. He pulled my panties down at the same time, and then I was bare before him, and Lee was on his knees in front of me. I looked down at him, at those wild eyes of his. I didn't care if this was a mistake.

I couldn't regret it. I couldn't have any more regrets. And then his mouth was on me, spreading my pussy wide as he sucked on my clit. I came right then, my whole body shaking, but he didn't stop. He kept eating me, licking and sucking and playing, and then he speared me with two fingers, working me. He met my gaze, and my knees nearly gave out.

He stood up then, kissed me hard, and I could taste myself on his mouth.

"Lee," I groaned.

"Shit, I don't have a condom." He nearly pulled away, and I gripped his hand, keeping him steady. I shook my head, my hand going beneath the waist of his jeans to grip him. He'd undone one button, making it easier, and we both froze.

"I'm clean," I whispered.

He studied my face, and I'd have done anything to know what he was thinking. That's why I didn't ask. "Me, too."

"And you can't get me pregnant again," I said into the silence as a bit of reality settled in.

Maybe we had both been laced with some drug, or he was feeling my hormones. I didn't care. This just didn't seem wrong. Why not? Why couldn't we do this?

And then he leaned back and stripped his shirt over his head. He was all long lines of muscle, the ridges of his abdomen forming an eight-pack. A tiny trail of hair ran from his belly button all the way down to below his pants, to where my hand currently stroked his cock. He rocked his body into me carefully, and I let out a shuddering breath as he pulled off the rest of my clothing. I couldn't breathe. Couldn't focus.

He palmed my breasts again, pinching my nipples, and then we were tugging on his pants, and he was toeing off his shoes. We hadn't moved anywhere, both of us still in the hallway, my back pressed to the wall. He palmed my ass, lifting me, and I wrapped my legs around his waist.

I met this gaze, his cock pressing against my entrance. "Lee."

"Paige."

Then there were no more words. He slid into me, my wet heat clamping around his dick, and I couldn't breathe. I was so sensitive, had always been, but even more so recently, and when he filled me to the hilt, him so deep within me, I knew I'd be sore tomorrow. I just kept kissing him, not wanting to think about the consequences of our actions.

We'd moved quickly up to this point, yet right then, Lee didn't move fast at all. He just met my gaze, and I couldn't stop looking at him. I couldn't stop looking at those hazel-gray eyes, ones that I had looked at for far too long.

I had always wanted Lee, and I had always told myself he was off-limits.

And yet, here he was, both of us coming together as we moved, the precipice changing with each instance.

And I knew this was wrong. He had promised to stay by my side through this new change in my life, and here we were, doing something we both knew would be an issue later, and yet I didn't want it to stop. I just wanted to be. I just wanted Lee for this instant. And when he moved again, turning to the side to walk me to the counter, his length still deep inside me, he set me on the edge of the island and continued to move, this time angling deeper. Far deeper than I thought possible.

He had one hand on my hip, the other behind my neck, keeping his thumb under my chin so our gazes clashed.

It was so intimate, so connected that I couldn't breathe.

This was my Lee.

And as I came, clamping around him, he filled me and kissed me again. And I reminded myself that he wasn't *my* Lee.

He was only my friend.

And this was a moment of insanity.

When he pulled out of me, and we cleaned up, he kissed me again, and I wondered why we had done what we'd just done. Why I was willing to risk everything.

He studied my face, and I saw the questions in his gaze. His phone buzzed, and he cursed. "It's Benjamin. I promised I'd stop by to watch the end of the game." He swallowed hard. "I need to go, but I'm going to buy that book. And then we'll talk."

"Talk," I whispered, standing there in my hastily redonned sweats as he finished dressing quickly. I was so lost, and I thought maybe the hormones had made me imagine everything that had just happened.

But he kissed me softly, then picked up his phone and walked away. We didn't talk about it. We didn't do anything.

But he'd said he would pick up the book.

So Lee wasn't going to leave altogether. He was only leaving now.

But again, we didn't talk.

CHAPTER 7

Lee

Somehow, for the last three months, Paige and I had done our best to pretend that nothing odd had happened. Considering that we were now sitting across from each other at one of our favorite cafés, one that had nothing to do with her ex, perhaps it had worked. After all, the more we didn't speak about the fact that I knew exactly how she tasted, precisely how she felt wrapped around me, the easier it was to pretend that maybe it'd never happened at all. Perhaps it was just a dream.

A vivid one where I could remember every single

inch of her as she pulsated around me. How her body shook as she came. The way her mouth parted ever so slightly, and she got that look in her eyes that told me she wanted it as much as I wanted her.

But again, we didn't speak about it.

Because that would require an awkwardness that neither of us could afford. I liked being near Paige. And, frankly, I wanted my skin intact. I had a feeling her brothers would skin me alive if they ever found out what we had done. And knowing her sister and the fact that they threw the word *castration* around willy-nilly, I did my best not to think about that, either.

"I think I should get a salad," Paige said as she leaned against the back of her chair. She had her hand resting on her stomach, and though she was just barely showing now, I couldn't help but smile.

"The baby wants a cob salad, then?"

She scowled at me. "I don't know what the baby wants. Probably fried chicken." She cursed under her breath.

I pressed my lips together so I wouldn't smile. "You want fried chicken now, don't you?"

She shook her head. "I always want fried chicken. And the biscuits that make your mouth dry but are still buttery at the same time and so delicious. No, I should eat a salad. It would be good for me."

"You're allowed to have fried chicken if you want,

Paige. You don't eat crazily every day. You're allowed to indulge yourself." As soon as I said the words, I knew I should have phrased it differently.

Her eyes darkened, and she met my gaze for an instant before shaking her head. "No, no indulgences for me. I need to be steady and smart about the choices I make."

I was going to pretend the pointed remark wasn't made toward me. And maybe it wasn't. Perhaps it was only about her food. But I didn't think so. Yet, how would I know? It wasn't as if the two of us talked about what had happened.

"Anyway. The spring salad with the peaches on it looks really good."

I looked down at the menu and nodded. "You're right. I was thinking about getting just a club sandwich."

"That sounds good, too. I'm starving."

"So you can keep food down today?"

She sighed. "That's the hope. I want to believe that I'll be like Brenna and only really have morning sickness in the first trimester. But considering my genes are the same as Annabelle's, we may be looking at a full pregnancy's worth of morning sickness."

"I can't wait."

I wasn't lying or being sarcastic. I liked being the one there for Paige. It gave me a sense of purpose that had nothing to do with work. Honestly, it wasn't something I could usually say when it came to my life. In the months since we'd found out about Paige's pregnancy, I'd kept to my promise. I tried to be there for her in any way I could. We were friends, first and foremost. And while we hadn't talked about that night in her kitchen, we were still there for each other, no matter what. I even went with her to her appointments if one of her siblings couldn't make it so she wasn't alone.

And we were becoming closer. We were friends. And it wasn't as if she'd completely closed herself off from her family. We still had Montgomery dinners nearly every week at one of her sibling's houses or her parents' house. I still went because I was a friend of the family. And, honestly, not many things had changed other than I sometimes held Paige's hair back for her, and I knew far too much about the first few months of pregnancy than I had ever thought I would know before this. Maybe from an outsider's perspective it was weird, but Paige didn't have anyone else to lean on. Yes, she could talk to her parents and her siblings, and any of the multiple cousins, but...

Her siblings were all dealing with things, between new babies and adoption processes. Archer was also a newlywed, so the family had a million other things to focus on, including Montgomery Builders and the expansion that would lead to bigger and more lucrative contracts soon. Paige was working double-time on that to get the deal done before the baby came, and I was just glad I could be there for her when I could.

"Can I have a bite of your sandwich?" Paige asked, fluttering her eyelashes.

I snorted and nodded. "Of course. And a plate of fries for the table."

"I'm getting a salad so I won't eat so much fried food." She scowled.

"The fries are just for the table. Meaning, I'll eat three-quarters of them."

"If you put fries on this table and eat three-quarters of them, I will stab you with my fork." She grinned as she said it, and I shook my head.

It felt as if we had been doing this forever. Yes, Paige and I had been friends for years, but it wasn't until recently that we had started to connect more. And not just because we had slept together. It was something more that I couldn't put my finger on. And for a man who'd sworn off serious relationships, that should worry me more than it did.

Once we gave our order, we leaned back in our chairs and talked. I was grateful that we were in the corner of the restaurant, out of the way. The place was busy, but we were secluded and off to the side, at our favorite table where it felt as if we could be alone and could talk about whatever we needed to.

Usually, these days, it had to do with the pregnancy, and I was fine with that because that's why I was here. To be her sounding board. Although, no matter how many pregnancy books I read, I still didn't feel like I was up to the task. Maybe by the birth, Paige would feel comfortable enough to lean into her family more. Because the Montgomerys weren't judging Paige, but Paige was judging herself and feeling lost because of the fact that Colton was still deciding what to do. And because that jerk was being the asshole he was, Paige was afraid to talk to her family about it. As if they would judge her. I didn't think they would. However, if I said something like that, Paige would push me away. So, I didn't say anything.

"I'm going to ask something, and you can't get mad." I looked at Paige as I said the words, and she narrowed her eyes.

"I don't think you can tell me not to get mad. I'm just saying."

"Fine, then please try not to get mad. How's that?"

"Decent." She paused, her shoulders hunching. "What is it?"

"Have you talked to Colton recently?"

She winced. And I hated myself. However, I wanted to know the answer. This relationship between her and me was odd and didn't make any sense on paper.

Colton was there. The ghost between us that wasn't so much of a ghost.

She sighed. "Not today. He texted to check on me yesterday, but his wedding is coming up next week, so he's a little busy with that."

I blanked. "He didn't invite you, did he?"

Paige rolled her eyes. "Of course, he did. Because he's Colton, and he never thinks about anything beyond wanting to do what he thinks is the good thing. I have no idea what he's planning. Or what he's thinking. Beyond the fact that he is starting his new life, but he also doesn't want to leave me in a bind. His words."

"I just don't know why you won't let me fly to him and beat him up."

"Because it's premeditated, and you'd end up in jail. Although knowing Colton, he would probably take it and wonder why on earth it took you so long for you to be a good guy and help me through some things." She rolled her eyes, and we leaned back as the waitress handed us our food. Paige immediately went for a fry, and I held back a grin.

"Don't judge me. But, oh my gosh, these taste so good." She made a mayo and ketchup concoction, and I held back a shudder before she devoured half the French fries and her salad. Since I was eating just as quickly, my stomach grumbling, we didn't need to talk too much.

By the time we were done eating and had updated each other on the next appointment that she had, as well as my job, her job, and the Montgomerys, my brain hurt. But this felt normal. Paige and I were dating and yet not dating. It didn't make any sense, but here we were. We weren't going to change anything.

"Do you want to go for a walk?" Paige asked, rubbing her stomach. "I think I ate too many French fries."

I nodded as I finished paying the check. "Yeah, a walk sounds good. I probably shouldn't have eaten all the bacon that came with that club sandwich."

"I think the waitress liked you. It was like double the meat." I waggled my brows, and she snorted. "That's not what I meant, but I get it. Now, is the park okay? That way, we don't have to move our cars."

"Sounds like a plan to me. Come on." I held out my hand, and she looked at it for a moment. I was afraid she would reject my offer and do her best to stand independent and strong, but Paige and I weren't like that. And I needed to remind myself of that. We may be ignoring the lingering tension between us, but we were friends. And we leaned on each other.

We walked our way through the park, the place relatively empty. It was a Thursday afternoon, and since I had worked the weekend to finish up a project, I had the day off. Paige had an appointment that morning and had worked over the weekend, as well, so her family had kicked her out of the office and said to enjoy some time off. I wasn't sure how Paige felt about that, but I knew it was strange. Everybody was so careful around one another. Things would likely blow up someday soon.

"What do you want to do for your birthday?" she asked after a minute, and I looked over at her. We weren't holding hands, just walking closely, but I still felt the warmth of her.

My stomach tightened as I processed her question. "I don't celebrate my birthday. Come on, Paige. You know that."

Only I knew she didn't know why. Only Beckett and Benjamin did. Not even Brenna. Though considering that Brenna had been part of our quartet for so long, it seemed like a lack of admission. I wasn't sure how to bring it up with anyone. And, frankly, I wasn't sure I wanted to.

"Why?" she asked softly. "Unless it's too much. You don't have to tell me."

I looked at her then and shook my head. "Considering I go with you to your prenatal visits, maybe I should tell you a little bit."

"Well, I wasn't going to bring that up. There are some lines."

I shook my head. "I don't celebrate my birthday

because my dad killed himself on my birthday." Paige nearly stumbled over her feet, and I cringed. "Sorry. I'm usually a little more subtle than that." I gripped her hand, keeping her steady.

She looked at me, her eyes filling with tears. "How do I not know that? I'm so sorry, Lee. What the hell?"

I shrugged, that familiar pain ebbing within me. I was used to the discomfort. It was what I was good at. "My dad wasn't healthy. He pretended that he was, but there was something wrong. He used to go to a therapist and be on meds, but he had schizophrenia. And no matter what we did, we couldn't fix him. It wasn't our job to fix him. But the system failed him, and maybe we did, too." I let out a breath. "I was fourteen. My dad shot himself in the head in his office while I stood in the doorway." I still remembered the sound of the gunshot, the way it echoed in the room and in my head. I still remembered the sight of the blood on the wall, the way half of my dad's head had blown off, his brains and whatever else splattering the desk. I remembered it all. Even now, I would do anything to forget.

We stood there, the two of us, Paige's tears freely flowing as her mouth gaped. "Oh my God. Lee."

I shrugged, knowing that it probably wasn't the right way to react. I wasn't sure what else to do. "He was sick for a long time. And while I'm glad he's not in pain anymore, I honestly don't think he even remembered what day it was or knew the room he was in. Mom sent me to go get him so we could celebrate my birthday. She didn't know what he was going to do, or the fact that I'd witness it." I swallowed hard, rubbing my damp palms on my pants. "She blamed herself. And it wasn't her fault. None of us could have guessed. When she asked me to go get him, I thought nothing of it. You see, he had been acting like my dad again up to that point. He had been smiling and coming to my games when I played soccer. He acted like he wasn't breaking from the inside. We didn't see it. My dad never hurt me. He always treated me well, even though he was sometimes a little distant. But something was wrong with him. And we couldn't fix it. And when it was too much for him, he killed himself. And I just happened to be there."

I let out a breath. "Mom died four years later. Not on my birthday, but close enough. We never celebrated my birthday in those four years, and it wasn't like she had the energy to do so when the cancer hit her hard. So, there's that. I became an orphan at eighteen, old enough to be an adult, but young enough to not know what the fuck I was doing." I shrugged, not knowing what else to say.

"Lee. I didn't know. I mean, I knew about your mother, but I didn't know anything else. I'm so sorry. I won't bring up your birthday, I promise."

I reached down and cupped her face. "It's okay. You didn't know. Beckett and Benjamin know because I got drunk and told them. They didn't understand why I didn't celebrate my birthday, either. You Montgomerys love celebrations."

She met my gaze, her lips forming a small smile that didn't reach her eyes. "Anything for cheese plates."

I leaned down, pressing my forehead to hers. She wore tall wedges today so I could reach her, and I appreciated it. "I'm okay, Paige. I went to a therapist. I still do, and I talk it out. I tried to figure out exactly who I blamed and all of that for so long. But I'm not that kid anymore. I had a long time to think about it, to come to terms with the demons my father couldn't face and couldn't fight any longer, even though he tried for so long. Paige, he tried. But in the end, it wasn't enough. And I understand that now. I'm not angry. It's the coincidence of it all that makes it a little too much."

"I'm sorry, Lee." Her fingers danced along my chin as she studied my face.

I sucked in a breath, not knowing what to say. "Schizophrenia shows in late teens and early twenties, according to most studies. I was always afraid that I'd follow in his footsteps. I'm past that age now, but I still see a therapist to talk things over. To see if there are any warning signs." She pressed her lips together, and I wiped away her tears. "Don't cry for me, Paige. I'm okay. I'll celebrate your birthday. This baby's birthday. Every single Montgomery birthday that there is so I can have my own cheese plates. But I don't celebrate mine."

"Well, then we need a holiday for you. What about Arbor day? Arbor day sounds nice."

I looked at her and ignored the little twist in my heart, the one that told me I wanted more. Only that wouldn't happen. The baggage we carried was far too much. I ignored it.

Paige smiled at me, then her eyes went wide, and she let out a groan.

"Paige?" I asked, alarm shooting through me.

"Something's wrong." she whispered, and then she doubled over in pain. She'd gripped her stomach, and I cursed under my breath, bringing her close, my heart racing.

"Paige."

"It's the baby. The baby."

She met my gaze, and fear coated my tongue, my worst nightmares were coming true.

CHAPTER 8

Paige

"I'm fine," I whispered once again as Annabelle tucked me into the couch. The blanket was soft and warm and the same one I had tucked around Annabelle when I brought it over when she hadn't been feeling well during her pregnancy. The twins had been hard on her, and while I had been going through my own issues at the time, I had loved how my big sister was married and having babies, and that my brother and his wife were having a baby at the same time. Although I had been jealous, to say the least, that everyone was moving on without me, I'd never resented who they were or what they were bringing to their lives. I was happy for them, and I had been then, too.

And now, Annabelle was here, taking care of me when I felt like shit.

"I know you're fine. But I want to take care of you. You're my sister. Let me love you." She whined the last words, her eyes dancing with laughter, but I saw the fear there, too. I was just as afraid, because I had almost lost the baby.

I'd had cramping, bleeding, and a scare that had nearly sent me over the edge. When I held myself, bending over in pain in front of Lee at the park, I had thought it was the end. That maybe my insecurities and worrying about how I'd fit into my family and how Lee or Colton felt about me had made me nearly lose this precious gift.

But Lee had carried me all the way to my car, ignoring the worried looks from strangers, and then had driven me to the emergency room. My obstetrician had shown up since she was in the same hospital and had told me I needed to rest for the next week. But I wouldn't be on permanent bed rest, not if she had anything to say about it.

I had smiled at that, even as fear erupted, taking my strength. However, I had to trust in her words that I would be okay.

And I hadn't been alone. Lee had been there. The worry etched on his face was something that would haunt my nightmares for years to come. But he had been there, had gotten me to the doctor, and had called my family. While a small part of me hadn't wanted to bother them, hadn't wanted them to deal with my issues, I was grateful.

Because I loved my siblings and my parents; they were everything to me. And though I was a stubborn asshole sometimes, I was grateful that they were there. And Lee had called them, knowing I would want them there, even if I wasn't fully cognizant of the decision because I was so scared.

"Thank you for being here," I whispered, and Annabelle looked up at me sharply, her eyes warming.

"I'll always be here for you, Paige. I know we're all a little busy with the upcoming projects, the expansion, and our own lives, but we're always here." She paused and sat down next to me. "And I'm glad that Lee is here for you, too."

I gave her a look and snorted. "You're not as subtle as you think you are in your questions."

"What? You two are just spending so much time together. For two people who are not together."

She studied my face, pressing her lips together. "We are not together," I said calmly. "We're just friends."

"Friends who have slept together at least once."

I blinked, looking up at my sister. "What?" I asked, my voice going high-pitched.

She just grinned. "You think I wouldn't know? Of course, I knew. I also know that you two are doing an excellent job of not talking about it and hiding what happened from the brothers. Not that I blame you. About the hiding part. You should probably talk about it, but I understand why you wouldn't. After all, you're pregnant, the father isn't in the picture—ish—and you and Lee have this weird friendship that seemingly came out of nowhere but I totally understand it."

"You said that all practically in one breath." I needed time to catch up on everything that she had just said. I could barely breathe, but here I was, doing my best not to stress out.

"I need to head into the office soon," Annabelle said after a minute. "But is there anything else I can get you before I go?"

I leaned forward and gripped her hand. "I'm okay, Annabelle. I just need to hang out on the couch here for a bit. I have food, books, my planner, and work. I'll be okay."

"You don't need to work, Paige," Annabelle began, and I shook my head.

"Let me work. You worked while pregnant. I can do the same thing."

"I suppose. But you don't have to."

"Well, what if I want to? I want to be a contributing member of this family. Don't forget that."

"Okay. I guess the good thing is the childcare part of the Montgomery Builders will be completely ready by the time you and the baby are ready to come back to work after your maternity leave."

I smiled. "I'm glad that we're following the other Montgomery footsteps in that."

"It makes sense to me. If all of us are starting the next generation nearly at the same time, we might as well make it easier for our employees. I'm sure Clay appreciates it, too."

Clay worked for Montgomery Builders under Beckett and had three kids of his own. Though they were a bit older, that didn't mean we didn't need child-care. Montgomery Builders, with the expansion coming up and hiring of new people, would now have a full, on-site childcare service.

It meant a lot of paperwork, and more issues than we previously had to deal with, but it was worth it. My parents started Montgomery Builders from their home, so we had always been a part of the place. Now, things were different, but only in that there were more of us, and we needed a bigger space. Mom had done most of the child-rearing since Dad was on-site most days, but for some meetings, Mom had to be there, and Dad had stayed home with a lot of us. I vividly remember those days before and after school, when we had taken care of each other, and things had gotten crazy. But it'd all worked out.

"I'm okay for the day. Thank you for everything."

Annabelle squeezed my hand. "I'm just sorry you had to go through that. I'm glad Lee was there."

I narrowed my eyes. "I don't know if you're trying to be comforting or fishing about Lee."

"I have twins, and I help run a very successful company with you. I can multitask."

I laughed, shaking my head. "Head into work. I'll be emailing you shortly."

"You do not have to work right now. The doctor says you should be careful with your stress."

"It's just emails. And I won't even send one that says, '*Per my previous email.*'"

Annabelle snorted and then picked up her phone. "Austin and Sierra may be stopping by later today if they get in on time."

I nodded, remembering that my cousin and his wife had planned to come up to Fort Collins to see us and had wanted to meet with me specifically. I loved my cousins, the huge family, and I knew that they were all worried about me. They had given me space, but as Austin was the eldest of us all, I knew he was probably coming to check on me.

"Are they coming here first or to Mom and Dad's?"

"Probably here because we love you." Annabelle kissed the top of my head and then headed out, leaving me alone on my couch for a bit.

My phone buzzed, and I looked at it, a small smile playing on my face as I did my best to ignore the feeling that filled me.

Lee: *I'm headed to a meeting, but I'll bring dinner?*

Me: *You're bringing dinner to a meeting?*

Lee: *Are you really correcting my grammar in a text?*

Me: *If I have to. I would say I'm bored, but this is the first time I've been alone in the past week.*

Lee: *Nobody's there with you? What the hell?*

I sighed, knowing he was only thinking of the baby and me.

Me: *Sierra and Austin are probably heading over in a minute. Or at least later today. I'm fine. Thank you for everything.*

Lee: *I'll check on you after I get out of the meeting. Be safe.*

I sighed, knowing we were both carefully not talking about whatever was going on between us. But I had *too* much going on; it would be confusing. I didn't want to lose Lee because I was stupid or making the wrong decision when it came to him.

Me: *Enjoy your meeting. Be smart as always. I'll be here.*

Lee: *Text me if you need anything. I'll answer. Always.*

I set my phone down and rubbed my temples, aware

that it might be smart to push him away, to make sure that we stayed in our respective bubbles and didn't cross any lines. And yet, we had clearly crossed a line before, but it wasn't like we could go back and not sleep together. It wasn't like I could go back and not want him the way I did and had. But it wouldn't be smart.

And I had done enough stupid things in my life. I didn't need him to be one of them.

I pushed all thoughts of Lee from my mind, knowing that no matter what I did, it would probably be the wrong decision, and I went to work. I had only gotten a few emails in when the doorbell rang. I sighed, knowing that it would be someone else here to make sure I was okay. What was wrong with me? I should be happy that I had so many people taking care of me, but all I could think about was that I was taking time away from their lives to help me. And I shouldn't be that person.

I got off the couch and made my way to the front door. I wasn't in any pain, and I was allowed to take short walks and move around. I wasn't on full bed rest. But I was so afraid that if I did something wrong, I would hurt the baby. Fear and bile coated my tongue, but I ignored it and looked through the peephole.

A big, bearded man with full-sleeve tattoos and a wicked grin on his face stood on the other side of the door, his petite bombshell of a wife next to him. There was also a very tall and muscular man beside them, and it took me a minute to realize that it was my nephew, Leif. I unlocked the door and opened it, my eyes wide.

"Since when do you have a man as a son, Austin Montgomery?" I asked, taking a step back as Austin let out a full belly laugh, although I was pretty sure he still had his eight-pack.

That was the Montgomery men. They lured women in with their looks and kept them with just being a Montgomery.

"Don't remind me," Sierra said softly as she walked in, her brown hair pulled back from her face with a cute headband. She kissed my cheek and then moved into the house, Leif and Austin following.

"Seriously, how are you like an adult?" I asked as Leif leaned down and kissed my cheek. The fact that he was nearly a foot taller than me just made me blink.

"I've been taller than you for a while now, Paige. Don't know why you just realized it." He winked, that dimple on his cheek making me roll my eyes.

"You're scaring me. You're like a full adult human person."

Leif beamed, looking even more handsome. I was honestly surprised he hadn't turned Austin's hair gray yet. "That's what happens with age. We grow up."

"Our other kids are down with my sister Miranda and her husband Decker," Austin explained as he hugged me tight, but not too tightly. As if he were afraid to break me. Then again, maybe he was. Not because of who I was, but because Austin was a big man. And the way Leif was filling out in muscle, he would be just as big as his father one day. It was crazy to think about.

"I'm sorry I couldn't see Colin and the twins."

"They wanted a cousins' day, and I wanted to spend some time with Leif out here and annoy your brothers. I figured we'd drop off Sierra just to hang out with you."

"Really? Without even asking?"

"I thought you told her that was the plan, Austin Montgomery," Sierra warned, her voice low.

I reached out and squeezed my cousin-in-law's hand. "I'm okay. Really."

"Well, good. We're here to bug you and just see how you're doing. We never really get to come up this way often."

"I've been looking at CSU, as well," Leif said, and I grinned up at him.

"Your gap year going well, then?"

Leif was eighteen, nearly nineteen now, and taking a gap year before college. The twins that Austin and Sierra had adopted after a long and arduous process had come into their lives recently. From what I heard, Leif had already been thinking about taking time off, and him wanting to be near his siblings during some of their first moments had only cemented the deal.

I loved how close they were, even if their family was a little different than the rest of ours.

Leif was from a relationship long in Austin's past. He hadn't even known his son existed until Leif was nearly ten years old or so. I wasn't sure of the entire story, but Leif had come into Austin's life around the same time Sierra had, and they had raised him together ever since. Colin had been born a couple of years later, and then the twins came a few years after that.

They were a blended family, but a loving one. And the two of them had each other through all of it. I also had my family, and I needed to remember that.

"Well, come on in and relax."

"Do you want me to get you anything?" Leif asked.

I raised a brow. "You are so like the other men in our family."

"What?" he asked, clearly confused.

I met Sierra's gaze, and she just grinned. "What Paige is saying, is that much like your father, you walk into any home and have to take over to make sure that everyone around you is safe and healthy."

"Why are you saying that like it's a bad thing?" Austin asked as he squeezed his wife. She rolled her eyes and rose on tiptoe to kiss his cheek.

"Nothing's wrong with that, Austin. I like it. We raised a good man."

"At least you're calling me a man now, Mom, and not a boy," Leif said with a roll of his eyes. He wrapped his arm around my shoulders and squeezed me to his side. "You're looking good, Paige. Are you through with the morning sickness part yet? Because that sucked when Mom got sick all the time."

Sierra just beamed at the fact that Leif had called her Mom, but I didn't comment on it. They'd had years of coming together as a family, and I loved how they interacted.

"I'm okay today, but we'll see."

"You should be sitting down, though," Austin growled, and I rolled my eyes, but since he was right, I went to the couch and held back a sigh as Leif and Austin both tucked me in.

Sierra shook her head, her shoulders shaking with laughter as she sat next to me. The two guys took up space in the armchairs, their shoulders so broad, I was afraid they wouldn't fit.

"Seriously, how are you all muscular? It's a little disconcerting."

"See? I told you that you bulked up this past year," Sierra said, clucking her tongue.

Leif just gave that Finn Ryder smolder. "The ladies like it, so I can't complain."

I met Sierra's gaze, and we both laughed before we talked about what was going on down in Denver and the expansion up here. The guys stayed for another hour, and Leif went into the kitchen to bring out iced tea for everybody. They weren't going to let me get up and take care of them, and since I really wasn't feeling like threatening my health just then, I let them. By the time Austin and Leif left, I was laughing so hard, it felt like a huge weight had been lifted off my shoulders.

"Thank you for letting us come and hang out with you for a bit."

I looked up at her and grinned. "Really? I don't mind."

"They're like mother hens, constantly helping out where they're sometimes not really needed."

I reached out and squeezed Sierra's hand. "They're good men. You've raised a good one."

"Sometimes, I feel like Leif showed up fully grown. He's so self-sufficient and amazing." She let out a breath. "We're also here because when something like this happens in the family, they tend to overreact and get scared." I froze as Sierra smiled softly, her eyes filling with tears. "Colin's birth was hard. I almost died, and I nearly lost the baby. And when I got pregnant a year later without even trying, I lost that baby during the second trimester."

My hands went to my mouth, my eyes stinging. "Sierra. I didn't know."

She grabbed my hand again and squeezed hard as she swallowed. "I don't need to tell you any of this if it's too much for you."

I shook my head. "No. I'm glad you're here. I'm okay, the baby's okay, but it's kind of hard to talk to Annabelle, Eliza, Brenna…any of them, when I don't know if I'm going to step on Eliza's toes or make Annabelle and Brenna worry about the fact that their pregnancies went off well."

Sierra nodded. "I know a little bit of Eliza's past, mostly because she and I talked about it." My eyes widened, and she smiled. "We don't tend to talk about loss or pregnancy pains, or how it feels to have a miscarriage. It's something we don't really discuss as women. And maybe we should. Our family has been blessed with procreation, whether it's adoption, multiples, or babies—all healthy and happy. We have been blessed, even with the heartache that sometimes comes with being married into this family, we have been blessed. But you know part of Eliza's story, and now you know mine. I lost a baby. We lost our little girl."

I choked off another tear, and she squeezed my hand again. "I will always remember Ashlynn. The name that we were going to give our daughter. And now I have two more babies, Gideon and Jamie, because their birth mother wanted them to have a different life. And we are trying to give them one they can thrive in. It's not what we planned, but it's who we are. And I want you to know, I know you're scared. I know that the unknown is around us, and you're afraid. At least given what we talked about on the phone. But I'm here for you. I don't want to be a family who keeps secrets and walks away from the hard things because it's scary. So, just know, I'm here."

I scooted next to her and held my cousin-in-law hard, both of us crying. "Thank you for trusting me enough to speak about it."

"As I said, I don't want the secrets. And it's something we need to talk about. About loss, about how it's not your fault. It is not your fault what happened. Just like it's not mine that we lost Ashlynn before we even got a chance to meet her. But it's okay. You're going to be okay. And I will always be here for you to talk about it."

So, I did. I spoke about nearly losing the baby, the fear, and how I was still afraid to do anything. Sierra listened, and we spoke. And by the end of the day, when Austin came up and took her home, I hugged my cousin hard, Sierra and Leif, as well, the knowledge in my nephew's eyes breaking a part of me but in the sweetest way possible. Because Leif must have been old enough to understand what had happened with his parents, and he had come today. Maybe not for college, but to visit. To hold me close.

And I knew I was damn lucky when it came to my family.

The doorbell rang soon after they left, and I opened it to see Lee. He had two bags of food in his hands and a worried look on his face. "I saw Austin and them leave. Are you okay?"

My tears had long since dried, the rest of my afternoon with Sierra and the others full of joy, and I just wrapped my arms around Lee tightly. "I'm okay."

He set the food down on the table next to me, closed the door, and held me tight. Then he lowered his head and kissed me softly. So softly. "Are you okay?"

I wasn't even sure he knew he had kissed me and what it might mean. Or the fact that we were so good about not talking about it.

"I am. I'm glad you're here. That...that you're my friend, Lee."

He gave me a shuttered smile, and I didn't know what it meant, but he held me close, and I held him right back.

Because we were friends. Nothing more, nothing less. But maybe exactly what we needed.

CHAPTER 9

Lee

Another month, another paper. The bane of my existence seemed to be my *only* existence these days. Months had passed since I'd finished the last one and yet, here I was, doing it again.

I rubbed my temples, staring at the words in front of me, wishing they would make some sense. It wasn't that I was necessarily bad at this. I just wished some things were slightly more manageable.

Andrea stood in the doorway, a stack of notebooks in her hand. "Are these what you asked for, boss?" she asked, and I rolled my eyes.

"Really? You're going to call me boss now?"

Andrea just shook her head and walked inside, setting the notebooks by the other stack already there. "I was trying it out. You're right. You're still just Lee to me. Sorry."

I grinned and leaned back into my chair. "Thank you for getting these. And for not calling me *boss*. Because I'm not your boss."

"True. Are you going to be staying here all night?" She glanced at my desk and at the stacks of papers, notebooks, books, and pamphlets around me.

I shook my head. "No, I need to go and help Paige with the crib once I get out of here. And probably pick up dinner because she'll want second dinner by the time I get there."

Andrea snorted. "I remember when I was pregnant with my kids, the first one I wasn't hungry by the third trimester unless it was for the cliches of pickles and peanut butter—just not together. And it was always at random times, like at two in the morning. And my husband would go out and get me anything that I wanted. He's pretty amazing."

I snorted. "I would have said he was amazing anyway, considering he could break me with his pinkie."

"He doesn't wrestle, or body build anymore, but he is still pretty fit," Andrea said with a wink, and I rolled my eyes. "Anyway, with our second, I was hungry all the time for anything and everything. Thankfully, I still ate decently healthy and tried to work within my portions so my doctor didn't rant at me, but all I wanted was food."

"I think Paige is in that area right now, considering she's due in a couple of weeks."

Andrea nodded. "Just don't tell her she's eating a lot, or she will hurt you, and you will probably deserve it."

"Like I would say that. What do you take me for? I'm the person who's bringing her food so she doesn't always have to cook."

"You're a good man, Lee. Especially to your... friend." She paused before she said the word *friend,* and I barely held back the urge to roll my eyes.

"We *are* just friends." Friends who had slept together. Ones who constantly gave each other looks and kissed each other gently, sometimes just to say hello, but just friends. Anything more would be a mistake; we both knew that. The baby was changing everything: how Paige felt, how we each thought about our futures. Paige's focus needed to be on the upcoming birth and being a single parent. I didn't need to be a part of that, messing things up with my needs and desires.

Andrea clapped her hands together, bringing me out

of my wayward thoughts. "Anyway, it's good that you're taking care of her."

I looked up as Andrea cleared her throat, her cheeks turning red. "Paige is pretty good about taking care of herself," I said drily.

"She doesn't have to do it alone." Andrea scowled. "I know I don't know the Montgomerys as well as you do. Just met them a few times in passing since you can't throw a rock without hitting one these days," she added with a laugh, and I snorted. "However, I'm still pissed off about what Colton did to her."

I held up my hand, shaking my head. "If we start talking about him, then I'll get growly, and I'm not in the mood to kick someone's ass. At least not when I have to get a few things done before I head out."

"You really are a good man, Lee Grier."

I shook my head. "It sure doesn't feel that way sometimes."

"You're wrong. You're a good man, and you're just going to have to deal with it."

"Um, thanks for that. And thanks for all of these books."

She smiled softly. "You're very welcome. Now go get everything set up so you can go and feed that girl of yours." I raised a brow. "Okay, maybe not that girl of yours."

I stared at her, and she just shook her head and left

me alone to my own devices, which was probably a mistake. I shouldn't be left alone with those. Not when I was always afraid of where my mind would go.

Andrea headed back to her desk, and I went back to work, pretending that I was okay, and that I wasn't thinking about Paige. But that was the problem. I had to work my ass off while I was here or work out so hard that I passed out in exhaustion afterward, so I didn't think about my best friend's little sister. Hell, she was my friend. I spent more time with her than I did with Benjamin or Beckett these days. Or even Brenna. They all had lives, problems, and families. And Paige was doing a damn good job of pretending that she didn't need anybody. Therefore, I just stepped in and didn't give her a choice.

I hadn't even been on a date in the past seven or so months. I paused as I looked down at my notebook, blinking. That couldn't be right, could it?

No, Leia had been the last person I went on a date with. And it hadn't even ended well, considering I left her standing in the rain. Or rather, she had left me standing in the rain because I wanted to help Paige. Not the best way to end a date, and I was probably a jerk for that, but then she hadn't wanted to help someone who clearly needed it. I shook my head, wondering why it even mattered.

All of my time off these days was for Paige and my friends. There was no time for sex, not since Paige.

I groaned. The last person I'd slept with had been Paige Montgomery. Something we were not discussing, even though we clearly should. I let out a breath and went back to work, focusing. I had gotten to work that morning at six, knowing I wanted to make it to Paige's home in time for dinner. I was working way too many hours, but then again, I always was. That was what I did, what I always did. I liked my job, but it was hard work. Maybe not physical, but mental. My brain was always going, trying to solve problems, attempting to figure out the next phase of what I needed to research and discover. To do that, I needed to work long hours. No wonder I wasn't dating. My work was my mistress, and Paige, well, Paige was Paige.

Not the most eloquent thing to say or even think, but it was the truth.

By the time my alarm buzzed, telling me I needed to get my head out of my ass and head over to Paige's after picking up dinner, I felt like my eyes were ready to bleed, but I was still jonesing. I loved my job. I loved science because there could be answers. Just like with math, there was always an answer. It might take me years to figure it out, but I would find it. There was always a chance for a new discovery. For taking things apart just to put them back together again. Nanotech was cutting-edge, and I loved what I did, even if it took all of my free time.

I made my way up front and noticed that Andrea was already gone for the day. I looked around and scowled, wondering why I was going home earlier than usual, but still one of the last people to leave. Only a couple of the postdocs were still here, as well as people finishing up any tests that were time sensitive. Still, though, I was doing this whole work thing wrong. I figured I didn't know how to take time off. Only I reminded myself, I liked my job. The more time I worked here, the less time I thought about Paige Montgomery.

I blinked once as I noticed my name scrawled on a notepad on the front desk, looking to see a note and a box of chocolates sitting there.

Lee, these came in while you were working, and I didn't want to bother you. Looks yummy. Andrea.

I shrugged, then opened the note in the small envelope that reminded me of something I'd seen before.

Roses are red

Violets are cute

Don't forget me

When the offer is moot.

I scowled, looked at the chocolates and the note, and shook my head. There was something seriously wrong with whoever was sending these, but I couldn't focus because who the hell would do something like this? I remembered the other note now, but while it looked the same, there was no way someone would be sending me a second one. I had never followed up on that first letter, but I needed to call my friend from college and see if they were the asshole. It didn't seem like a Montgomery prank, but who knew these days. So, I'd ask them, too. I moved the note and gift to my desk and figured I'd take care of it in the morning. Just then, my phone buzzed.

Paige: *I think I'm supposed to only eat bland food tonight. I'm sad.*

My lips twitched.

Me: *Salads it is.*

Paige: *If you bring a salad into this house, I will murder you.*

I just shook my head and headed out to my car.

Me: *You will be eating a salad because the doctor said you need more veggies. But I was thinking of Southern food. Just not Cajun with the actual spices.*

Paige: *Gravy. Yes. Bring me all the gravy. Now I'm drooling.*

I laughed, set my phone on the center console, and headed to go pick up our dinner and go to Paige's.

I knew what Andrea and the others at work thought. That Paige and I were together, or at least tiptoeing around it. But we couldn't be. Paige would be a mom and needed to focus on that part of what her future entailed. I wouldn't be that part.

I had to let her become who she needed to be. And no matter how much I wanted her, it was the fucking wrong decision.

As it was, her brothers didn't know we had slept together. And they would never know. I was pretty sure they only let us hang out as much as we did because they thought everything was platonic. Not that Paige would allow her brothers to take over her life, but they weren't interfering much with anything these days because I was here. I was helping. Or at least, I was pretending.

It was complicated, a mess, and I had no idea what I was doing, but Paige wasn't mine, and I had to remember that.

I picked up our dinners and told myself I should probably learn a few skills when it came to cooking. Paige was a much superior cook than me, and I needed to be better so I didn't spend so much time and money picking up food orders. But between work and helping get Paige's house ready for the new baby, I wasn't the best person for cooking.

I pulled into Paige's driveway, then let myself in with the key she had given me. It was probably weird that I had a key, but I wasn't going to complain. It made things easier.

"Paige? I have dinner."

"I'm in the nursery. Why is this crib evil?"

I scowled, set our dinner on the kitchen island, and stomped towards the nursery. Paige sat on the floor, pieces of the crib strewn about her, and instructions on her calves. Considering she was nearing the end of her pregnancy and twice as large as she had been even a month ago, I could not believe she had even gotten herself down onto the floor. I wasn't going to mention that, though, because I liked my balls exactly where they were, thank you very much.

"What the fuck are you doing?" I asked, surprised at the venom in my tone.

Paige's eyes widened. "I'm putting together my crib. I can do this."

"I'm sure you can, you're a Montgomery, and you have builder's genes, but why the fuck are you on the floor?"

She blushed. "It seemed like a good idea at the time. But now I can't get up, and I have to pee. So, yes, I need your help. Damn it."

I scowled and then went behind her, putting my arms under her shoulders, my hands on her hips as I gently boosted her up. She grunted, and I hated that I loved the way she felt against me. There was something seriously wrong with me, considering all I could do was think about bending her over and fucking her, and she was nearly nine months pregnant.

"I hate that I can't do things on my own."

I turned her in my arms and cupped her face. "You do everything on your own. You're damn good at it. Stop."

"I can't stop. Colton isn't coming. He made a decision that he's going to stay where he is, and here I am. Alone."

I ignored the fire inside me at those words. Every time Colton called these days, Paige ended up in pain, and I hated the other man. Though I hated him more because he had that connection that I would never have, and it had taken me far too long to realize that. "And what am I? Chopped liver?"

Her eyes filled with tears, and I hated myself. I leaned down and did the one thing that both of us never talked about.

I kissed her.

"I have to pee," she mumbled against my lips, and I snickered and let her go.

"Don't put that crib together without me."

"I just might. Because there's no way you're bending down to help. Not with that waddle of yours."

She flipped me off, then closed the bathroom door behind her. And so, I leaned against the doorjamb, crossing my arms over my chest, and wondered what the hell I was doing.

I had offered to help her through this because we were friends, and I hadn't known what else to do. But now, there was no going back. Yet, there wouldn't be any moving forward, either.

Not when it came to Paige or the life we had chosen to live, however tangled, messy, and confusing it was.

CHAPTER 10

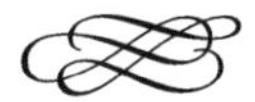

Paige

"I'm so glad that you have a pop of bright color in your theme," Annabelle stated as she leaned down and kissed the top of my head. I looked up at my sister and shook my head.

"Well, purples and grays and a little bit of yellow for bumblebees sounded good to me."

"While I love the aesthetic of farmhouse gray and all of those Instagram-worthy nurseries, I kind of miss the Crayola-looking painted rooms," Eliza added as she brought in a tray of finger sandwiches.

I looked around at my sisters, biological and

married-in, and just grinned. "I thought about it. But I love purple. I hope this little one wants purple, too. If they choose a different color, then we'll go with that one."

"I love that you're going to be surprised with the sex of the baby," Brenna added as she checked her baby monitor.

Rafael, as well as Annabelle's twins, were sleeping upstairs in the nursery in Annabelle and Jacob's home. The guys had all offered to take their kids for the day, but I wanted the babies here. What was a baby shower without babies? And not just my upcoming one. A few of my friends from college, around the city, and those that worked for the Montgomerys were also here. Thirty or so women who all wanted to be part of the day. I still couldn't believe that the time was here. Soon, I'd be holding my baby—a single mother who worked far too many hours but was ready. Or at least I was as ready as I could be.

"This entire adventure has been a surprise. Why not one more thing?" I winked as I said it, and the women around me laughed. I had invited my brothers, Jacob, Lee, and a few other guys, but they had all begged off, saying they had other things to do. I had just rolled my eyes at them, knowing they were being weird about it. Of course, they had come to Brenna's baby shower, and when they were forced to play baby games, I had a feeling they'd all decided they wanted nothing to do with it. I didn't mind, though. It was nice seeing everybody, including how my mom was in her grandmotherly bliss.

I was surprised that Archer wasn't coming, though. He usually came to things like this, mostly because he loved parties and being around our family. But he hadn't shown. He rarely did these days, and that worried me, but it was fine. I wasn't going to think too hard about it.

"Okay, now we're going to play the normal games because I didn't have time to research anything more unique. So, no saying the B-word," Annabelle said, clapping her hands together. My mom rolled her eyes and started handing out clothespins.

I just snorted but played along.

"I made cupcakes," Brenna put in as she gestured towards the table laden with food and sweets. There was a present table on the other side, my nursery registry nearly cleaned out. It made me want to cry, my eyes stinging as I thought about it. There were so many people that cared, and it surprised me, but it shouldn't.

I was the one who kept people at a distance. I didn't want to rely on anyone because I didn't want to take time away from them. Only I had taken time from Lee. Maybe that was a good thing. I still didn't know what we were doing, other than being careful about not doing anything at all.

And soon, I wouldn't be able to blame the hormones.

"What kind of cupcakes?" I asked, pushing all thoughts of Lee and Archer and my problems out of the way.

"Mostly lemon drizzle, but also a strawberry cream."

"I think I'm going to pass out," Andrea teased, and I smiled over at the other woman. She worked with Lee, and I spoke to her often since she answered the phones if Lee couldn't. When I ordered in lunch for Lee, I usually sent in a plate for her, as well. Lee took care of me, so I did my best to take care of him. It was my job at Montgomery Builders. I made sure that my family ate, made their appointments, and scheduled the hundreds of consults we had each month. I was good at my job, and I enjoyed it. If I could help Lee out, as well as his team, I would.

It was nice seeing her there, even though we didn't know each other that well. It seemed like the pregnancy brought people together, even when I wasn't prepared.

"I have been waiting for this moment for months now," my mom said as she leaned forward and took my hand. "I love you, honey."

I looked over at her and smiled. "What moment?" I asked, and then she looked over my shoulder. I was a little too big to turn completely. Annabelle, Brenna, and Eliza walked into the room again, each of them holding a bundle.

"I've been busy puttering away, but I couldn't wait for you to see this."

Mom stood and rubbed her knee, and I squeezed her hand. "Is your knee hurting you?" I asked.

Mom just patted my hand. "Old age. It happens. Especially when you're carrying around sets of twins all the time."

"I feel like you're blaming us," Annabelle said as she leaned forward and kissed Mom's cheek. "Okay, Paige. We have games, food, and just a fun afternoon planned, but first, we can't wait. You have to see these."

I looked at the bundles, and tears slid down my cheeks.

"Damn hormones," I grumbled, and everyone in the room laughed.

Brenna handed me the first bundle, and I gently unwrapped it.

"Oh my gosh," I whispered. I pulled out the lavender and gray blanket and tried not to cry on it.

Brenna leaned forward, her eyes bright. "You did such a fantastic job knitting our blankets when we were pregnant that I did my best with this one. And my sisters helped me. They're much better at knitting, so when they came to visit, we worked together."

The blanket was so soft. I knew that I would treasure it always. I swallowed the lump in my throat, trying to catch my breath. "I can't believe it."

"You're family. We want you to know that we love you, and we cannot wait to meet the newest Montgomery."

Because the baby would be a Montgomery. Colton would have some visitation rights, but he didn't want to ruin my life. At least, that's what he had said. That he would pay child support and visit when he could.

I wasn't going to ask for full parental rights. I wouldn't ask him to sign them over to me. Because I couldn't do that to the baby or to Colton. But I *was* on my own. Colton would send money and would show up occasionally, but he had his own life, a wife, and a job he loved.

And only a few ties in Colorado.

I pushed those thoughts from my mind, not wanting to worry about the things that would break me until later. Instead, I tried to get up to hug Brenna, but Brenna pushed me back down, kissed my cheek, and hugged me tightly. "We love you, Paige," she whispered and then moved back. Eliza handed me the next bundle, and I gave her an odd look.

"What is this?" I asked, shaking my head.

"Open it, silly."

And so I did, promptly bursting into tears. Little

gray and purple and bumblebee knitted booties, a sweater, and little caps that ranged in sizes so the baby could grow into them.

"You did all this?" I asked, swallowing hard.

"My brothers and I did, actually," Eliza hedged, and the room quieted as they looked at her.

"My brothers just got out of the military and needed something to do with their hands, so they're learning to group knit. I don't ask questions, but they are having fun with that and crocheting. The fact that they could do the little booties like that while I couldn't worried me, but those are my brothers. Good at everything they do." Eliza rolled her eyes, and I held the little knitted booties close to my chest.

"Your brothers are freaking amazing. Hot, single guys with good jobs who can also knit? Why don't they live here?" I teased, and Eliza just radiated.

"Oh, I'm sure a few of them could move up here if that's what you need." She winked as she said it.

I blushed, shaking my head. "No, I think I'm going to have enough on my hands."

Andrea met my gaze, and I shushed her. My family didn't know what was going on with Lee and me, other than that no one knew what was going on with Lee and me, let alone us. But Andrea had always had a feeling. Probably because I talked with her when I tried to take care of Lee the way he took care of me.

She had an inkling that something was going on, even though nothing was. It couldn't. Not when we were both doing so well at not letting things happen like that.

Annabelle handed me the last package. When I opened it, I swallowed hard, emotions and hormones choking me.

"Mom and I made this," Annabelle said as both my mom and sister reached forward, their hands entwined with mine.

"It's a quilt made of your baby clothes and a few other things I kept. You were the fifth child, Paige. And though people joke that those never get the baby books or the new clothes and always get hand-me-downs, and while that might have been somewhat true, I always kept things I wanted to give you for this day. You are a light and joy in my life, Paige. And I cannot wait to see and meet this new Montgomery of ours. You are so strong, so able. You're going to be an amazing mother. I love you, baby."

"What she said," Annabelle whispered, and then I was crying and laughing. Thankfully, one of my friends from college giggled loudly into her champagne and set down the glass.

"Half a glass, and I'm already too buzzed. Is there a special Montgomery wine I don't know about?"

Annabelle snapped her fingers. "You know, that is

something we haven't started yet. We need a Montgomery vineyard."

"Maybe I can convince my brothers down in the Hill Country in Texas to begin a Wilder Wines. That would be fun."

"Now I want wine," I grumbled and shook my head, letting Annabelle take the bundles away. I snacked on sandwiches, played baby games, and couldn't help but think about how my life wasn't exactly what I had planned.

I would never regret this. I couldn't because I was about to hold my baby. I would be a mom. It didn't seem real, and it might not truly feel that way until I held my child. However, I was here. I wasn't going anywhere. And I was doing this alone, somewhat. I had my family, I had my friends, and they would always be here for me. Lee would always be there for me.

But this wasn't exactly how I had planned my life. Yet, I couldn't change it. And I wouldn't. I just needed to remember that, even if I had to remember not to think about Lee because he was just a friend. Only my friend.

As my hand itched to call him, to text him photos of the day, I didn't. I would show him later, but I wouldn't rely on him just now. Soon, he would need to walk away. He would remember that he had his own life, and being the guy who was always there for someone he didn't want to be with in that way wasn't his future. I needed to remember that.

Lee wasn't mine. And I was my own person. I had all I needed.

I just needed to believe that.

CHAPTER 11

Lee

I'd had a long morning at work, even though it was a weekend, and I probably should have taken the day off, but I couldn't sleep. I kept thinking about the notes and Paige, and the fact that I didn't know what was going to happen next. I wasn't even sure why I had been targeted or who could be sending the notes and gifts to me in the first place. I'd had a few girlfriends in the past, but none that would do something like this.

Ashleigh had been sweet but wanted someone to travel the world with her. I was a relative homebody, despite never actually being at home because of work and Paige these days. Justine was an attorney who had moved to New York, and I'd figured we'd ended things on good terms. I'd dated Caroline for a few months, but she'd told me that she couldn't be serious about me. She worked longer hours than I did at a security company at their front desk, and we rarely went out, but I'd always been exclusive regardless. I'd only had a few dates with Leia, and though it had ended oddly, especially in light of her coming over like she had, I wasn't sure who else it could be—even if I didn't think it was her at all.

It could be anyone from work, my past, or even someone I'd walked by on the street that decided to do this. I hadn't gotten another note since the one that came with the chocolates, but I'd kept it. I wasn't even sure what to do about it. When I called my friend from college, he had thought I was insane by even asking. We'd all grown up. And it honestly wasn't something that he would normally do. So, I had laughed it off, yet worry still settled in my gut.

It was odd. I didn't know what it all meant. So, I had worked that day, and now I was going to Paige's, something I did more often than not.

If a day ended in Y these days, I went to Paige's house. Today, it was for lunch, something I would be making and not bringing over. We had both promised that we'd get better at cooking. For the baby. Not that I would be living with her or helping her raise said baby. I was just here for the pregnancy. And then I would walk away.

I frowned as I pulled into the driveway.

"Walk away?" I whispered. That didn't sound right. I supposed I would help her when she needed me. It was what I was doing now. When would it be too much? When would I want more?

Or, at least, more than I already had.

Paige opened the door as soon as I got out of the car, and I grinned. "Waiting for me, are you?"

She rolled her eyes. "I made salads."

"I thought I was cooking," I said as I walked up to her and kissed her cheek. It was just something we did now. Normal. It wasn't weird.

It was totally weird, and I was probably messing everything up, yet I didn't know what else to do. We acted like a couple who wasn't a couple, but I didn't want to ask her about it, either. I didn't want to talk to her about it. Because if I did, she would get stressed out, and she was ready to have the baby any minute now. I did not want to be too much for her.

Her eyes warmed as she peered at me, and I tried not to look too much into it. It was getting harder and harder to do these days. "All I did was take a bagged salad, a rotisserie chicken, and call it a day. I don't know if that counts as cooking."

"It's still closer than all the takeout we've been having." I pulled off my jacket and set my phone on the table. "I know you can't have any cheese or anything right now, but do you want something other than the salad?"

Paige shook her head. "No, I think I got heartburn last night from dinner. I don't know. It's annoying because I can't tell if it's from food, the baby, or just me stressing about food and the baby."

I reached out my hands and raised my brow. "May I?"

Paige grumbled. "You know you don't have to ask to touch my stomach. Yes, the rest of the world does, but you and my family do not. Mostly because I'm tired of saying yes. I like when you say hi to the baby."

I couldn't help but smile. "I like when I say hi to the baby, too." I leaned down, pressing both hands to her stomach. The baby kicked, and I grinned. "Hello, there, little rock star."

"Do you think she's going to be a rock star?"

"I think they could be anything he or she wants to be."

"I keep thinking it's a girl in one minute, and then maybe a boy. I don't know. It'll be fun to see what happens. You know, after the whole scariness of childbirth and pain and screaming and crying and everything else that happens wears off."

I shuddered. "I was at that child birthing class with you and Annabelle. Or the end of it, at least. I remember what happens. I saw the video."

Paige cringed. "Don't remind me of that."

I snorted. "Shouldn't I? You're the one who's about to go through that."

"I'd like to go into this thinking that it's not going to be painful. That I just go through it, and some form of endorphins make me forget."

"Is that really how that happens?"

"I don't know. But if I'm going to pretend, then I'm going to make sure I live in this blissful harmony."

"Anything you need." I pressed a kiss to her belly and then to her cheek. There was something seriously wrong with me if I was torturing myself like this. But Paige kept looking at me, kept kissing me back, so maybe we were good at living in denial. It was a peaceful place.

"What are we doing, Lee?" she asked, and I froze, surprised she'd asked the question.

"What do you mean?" My heart nearly stopped, and I tried to act casual, though I knew I was failing.

"You know what? What *are* we doing? You're here every day. You've gone to birthing classes with me."

Panic sliced through me. "Because we're friends." Not quite a lie.

"Are we? The rest of the family is too worried about stressing me out, so they're not even asking about how weird the situation is. We're not talking about the fact that we had sex, Lee. I've only had sex with three people in my life, and you were the third person. I can't believe we're not talking about it."

It took me a minute to catch up to the information, and I blinked. "Only three?"

"Yes. Only three. Look at you go. You're one of the few."

"Paige. I thought we decided that talking about it or dealing with it would be too much during the pregnancy and while you were dealing with Colton."

"Really? Or is that just what we said to each other because it was easier?"

"Maybe." I ran my hands through my hair. "I don't know, Paige. Hell. We spend all this fucking time together, and I love it. I love hanging out with you. I love that I'm part of this, even in a weird way."

"But what is this? The pregnancy? The baby? Are you here for more? And, yes, this is probably the worst time to be asking these things, but I think I need to know. I'm so scared, Lee."

I reached for her, cupping her face. "Don't be scared. I'm here."

"But isn't that the problem?" she whispered, and I took a step back, feeling as though I'd been hit.

"It's a problem that I'm here?"

"That's not what I'm saying at all. I think it's a problem that we don't know what we're doing. We're living in this bubble, like we can just be friends. But we're constantly touching one another, forever leaning on one another. We kiss all the time, Lee. And we're so good about pretending that it doesn't mean anything. But what if it does?"

I cursed under my breath. "You're right. What if it does? But is this the right time to think about it?"

"When will be the right time? I've got eighteen years of raising this baby, and what happens after that? What do we do after that? Is that when we finally talk? When my child is so confused as to who you are in their life that they don't know whether to call you Uncle Lee or Daddy?"

I swallowed hard, the words twinging more than they should. "I don't know."

"I don't know either. I'm so afraid we're going to hurt each other and this baby because we're terrified of losing one another or actually talking about the important things. And I've waited way too long to have this conversation with you. I've been so afraid, Lee. But here we are. I'm going to have a baby soon. My due date is in two weeks. I don't know who you are to me. Other than the person that I care about more than anyone. Because you are always there, you make me smile, you make me laugh, and you're here for me. You've always been there, but I don't want to force you into being something you're not."

Shock radiated through me, and I stared at her. "What would you be forcing me to do, Paige?"

"I'm a ready-made family. I'm not just your best friend's little sister. I'm going to be a mom. I come with baggage."

I shook my head, wondering how she could think that. I was the damaged one. Not her. "You know my baggage, Paige."

"Exactly. You told me outright when you said you would help me through this pregnancy because I needed someone to lean on, that you didn't want a family. Marriage and kids weren't in the game for you. And so, what does that mean? What does that mean for us if this baby isn't what you were thinking of for your future? Because that's what I have. We have been so good about not talking about what is important that we missed the most important thing. I don't want to pull you down into a life that you didn't ask for. But I don't know if I can let you go, either."

I sighed and cupped her face. "I never wanted to pressure you."

"Same here. But I think we messed up by not talking

about it long before this. Because watching you go will break me, Lee. And I don't know what that means. I don't know what I feel because I feel so many things all at once. You have no idea what it feels like to have a thousand emotions and hormones hitting you one after another, and I can't even focus. I can't breathe."

I sighed and leaned forward. "That's why I've been saying we should wait."

"Wait for what? For my baby to walk towards you instead of me the first time? For you to capture their first steps on video? Or what? Have their first word be *Daddy* as you hold them? It's not fair to you or this baby for us not to have answers, and yet we have no answers. I don't even know what's going to happen with Colton."

"Don't say his fucking name around me."

"Well, what am I supposed to do? Technically, he is the father. Why couldn't Colton just be great and make things work?"

I felt like she had kicked me, and as her eyes widened, I knew she regretted the words. "Let's not fucking talk about Colton right now."

"I'm sorry. I didn't mean that you were stepping into Colton's shoes even though some think you are, but you're not. It's more of things being so backward, and this isn't what I wanted."

"This isn't what you wanted," I repeated.

She threw her hands in the air as I tried to process

her words. "No, I wanted things to be easy, even though life is never easy. And things are far different than I ever thought possible."

I shook my head. "Just because it's different doesn't mean it's wrong."

"I want to believe that. But I feel like I'm trapping you in this with no end in sight." She bit her lip, her eyes filling.

I took her hand, needing her touch and knowing this conversation was far overdue. "I don't know why you would feel that way."

"Because it's the truth. You came to me because you saw me crying in the rain, and then I never let you go."

"Or maybe I just didn't leave."

"I hate him," she whispered.

"Colton?" I swallowed hard, trying to catch up.

"I hate him so much. He's happy out there and stringing me along because I don't want my child to feel neglected. And it makes me think that I have the worst taste in men."

"You slept with me, Paige. I can't say that you have the worst taste."

She shoved at me half-heartedly. "But you don't want a family."

"I didn't before..." I said out of the blue, and she stared up at me.

"What?"

"I didn't want a family I could lose. And that's what I told myself. What if I were to fall in love, have a baby, have a family? And I ended up like my dad. It doesn't make any sense, but that's what I always had in my head. So, when I said that none of that was in the cards for me, that's what I pictured. But we're not that cookie cutter. We're far from it."

"Lee."

"Shh," I whispered, putting my finger to her lips. "I don't want to say we start over, but maybe we talk to one another. I don't want you to hate me like you hate Colton. But I haven't run away yet. I've been here through all of it. Through the cravings, the setting up your baby shower with your sisters, through dealing with the odd looks your brothers give me because they don't know where we stand. I've been through all of it. Through your mood swings that led to my mood swings," I joked, and she pushed at my arm.

"Watch your step."

"See? Mood swing."

"Lee," she whispered.

"Just don't hate me like you hate him." And then I leaned forward and cupped her face. Our bodies were touching, the baby kicking against my stomach, and I knew this was wrong. This was the wrong time. It always had been. Because before Paige was with Colton, she had been off-limits. And then after, she was pregnant, and both of us had done a very good job of not fucking things up.

Yet it had always been too much.

And then, I didn't want to walk away. But I also didn't know what any of it meant. When she parted her lips, and I lowered my head, making another mistake I knew we would have to get through, she moaned.

Then she gripped my waist, and I kissed her hard, each of us groaning into one another.

"I should blame this on the hormones," she whispered.

"So are hormones catching, then?" I teased and kissed her again.

"We really need to talk about what we're doing."

"We will. Later."

She kissed me again, and I kissed her back, knowing that this was the worst decision we could be making. We'd been so close to discussing who we were to each other, and then those fucking emotions.

Only when she put her hands on my chest and pushed me away, I took a step back, my eyes wide.

"Paige? What is it?"

She put her hands over her belly, her eyes wide, her face going pale. "My water broke."

I looked down at her feet, and then up at her face, and the ground fell out from under me.

CHAPTER 12

Paige

Fear cascaded down my spine, and I gripped Lee's hand. He looked over at me before he returned his gaze to the road, going the exact speed limit.

I breathed through the pain, grimaced, and couldn't help but smile at him. "You're not even going to go five over, are you?" I asked with a laugh.

We stopped at a traffic light, and he raised his brows at me. "Of course, not. I've seen those movies. They get pulled over, and then they have to explain to the cop that you're having a baby. And then either you have the baby right then and there—and I'm not in the mood to deliver a baby in a car. Or we go speeding at seventy miles an hour around curves following the cop as he blares his lights. The traffic here is insane, Paige Montgomery. We are not risking that."

I looked over at him then, my heart doing that little shuddering thing. It was so hard to think when he was so fucking perfect.

"You're panicking." My stomach felt like it twisted, and I did my best to remember my breathing from our classes. Annabelle had been so soothing during all of them. Had rubbed my back. Had explained to me how her birth had gone. She had started with an epidural, but it had only lasted for part of the birth. So, she'd been able to feel nearly everything both times, and my brain shorted out just thinking about it.

"Of course, I'm freaking out. You're giving birth. It's a big thing."

I ignored that little clutch in my heart and squeezed his hand tightly. He was driving one-handed and doing well with it. I needed his touch, though, and I was greedy for it. In the middle of labor was the one time I would allow myself to be needy.

It was a decent excuse anyway.

"And you called your family?"

I smiled. "Yes, the only problem is they're in Denver."

Lee practically swerved off the road, and I winced. "Why are they in Denver? You're near your due date. They should know to be here."

I sighed, rubbing my belly as I did some slow breathing through a contraction. The contractions were coming closer and closer together, and I didn't want to think too hard about that. I couldn't help but remember the pain, the bleeding that had happened when we'd had that scare at the beginning of the pregnancy. Speaking with Sierra and Austin and even Leif had helped right after everything happened, but I still woke up in the middle of the night drenched in sweat and scared. I'd only texted Lee once, and that had been after the first time. He had come over and held me. I hadn't texted him after that.

It wouldn't be fair to either of us. But he was so caring, so wonderful. He spoke to the baby as much as I did, and I had no idea what we would do once I held my baby for the first time. Once he did.

Because in my head, he was still going to walk away. He was always going to continue his life, and I would do this alone. Yet that was so stupid.

So freaking stupid. But I didn't know what I was supposed to be doing.

"Why are they in Denver?" he asked again, and I brought myself out of my thoughts, the ones that wouldn't leave me quite yet.

"It's Austin's birthday. I didn't go because I had an appointment this morning, remember?"

I did. "Shit. I knew about the birthday. Wasn't I invited?"

My lips twitched. "You were. But you said you had to work. Because you took time off to take me into the hospital earlier on Monday for my appointment."

"Oh, right. Is your family on their way?"

"Yes, but there is tremendous traffic on I-25, and there's an accident. They'll get here." They *had* to get there.

I fisted my hands over my belly before I forced myself to relax and rubbed circles over my stomach. "Everything's going to be fine. They're going to get here. The baby will be fine, we're going to be fine, and you are almost at the hospital. You're doing great."

He gave me a look. "You're placating me, but I appreciate it. I didn't realize I would be the one to panic here."

"Honestly, neither did I."

My phone buzzed, and I held it in one hand while Lee kept my other hand secure.

Annabelle: *We're driving as quickly and as safely as we* *can, but I-25 North is jammed. Traffic is blocked for miles. We're going to make it. We love you.*

Eliza: *My brother Evan is at the house if you need him. I can text him. He can be there.*

I laughed and shook my head.

Me: *Thank you. You'll be here. I know you will. Don't worry. And I don't need Evan here. I don't know Evan.*

"What are you laughing about over there?" Lee asked as I breathed through the pain once more.

"Eliza is asking if her brother Evan can come and join me in the delivery room because I don't think my family's going to make it." My voice went high-pitched at that point, and Lee's eyes widened before he turned into the hospital parking lot.

"What?"

I explained about the accident as my phone continued to buzz, everybody who wasn't driving giving me updates.

Me: *Getting into the hospital now. Text Lee. Or have him join this group chat.*

Lee's phone began to buzz, and he narrowed his eyes at me. "Was I just added to the Montgomery family group chat?" he asked with a growl as he jumped out of the car. He had parked, and I was grateful for that. I didn't want him to have to drop me off and leave me alone. I probably should be okay with being alone at this point, but I couldn't care about that right then.

"Come on, Paige. Let's get you inside. We're going to meet the baby."

My eyes widened as I waddled next to him, breathing slowly. He had found a place to park only three spots away from the door, so it was an easy walk that honestly helped soothe some of the pain. We walked in, and then I bent over, letting out a pained groan as Lee rubbed my back and called out over my head.

"Help. Somebody. She's in labor. Her water broke. And we're going through contractions less than a minute apart at this point."

"You were counting even as we were driving?" I ground out.

"Of course, I was. I'm your birthing partner. Well, your backup for Annabelle, but where is Annabelle?"

Everything moved quickly after that. I was admitted and barely into a dressing gown when I screamed, begging for an epidural.

"I'm sorry, Paige, you're too close to the end for the epidural. We're going to have to do this according to a different birthing plan."

I looked up at my doctor, the one who had helped me through everything, even through the near loss and finding out that I was pregnant in the first place. I swallowed hard. "What do you mean I'm not getting pain meds?"

"We're out of the window where it's safe, but that means we are closer to having your little one here. You're doing great. I am going to be right back. The nurses will be here with you. And you're not alone." She looked over her shoulder as Lee paced near the doorway, his hair standing on end from as many times as he had run his hand through it.

"You're saying she doesn't get to have an epidural?" His voice dropped at that, and I didn't blame him, panic sliding up my spine along with the pain.

"No, I'm sorry. Ice chips alone. Take care of her. I know you know the drill. I'll be right back."

"You're going to leave us alone?" I asked, my voice going high-pitched as I gripped Lee's hand in earnest. He squeezed right back, and I leaned into him, my body shaking.

"You two have each other. You're not alone. And soon, baby will make three." She was so calm as she said it, and I knew she was trying to soothe me, but I wanted to throttle her. Or throw something. Yes. Throw something.

Nerve-racking pain shot up my spine, and my hips vibrated as if something were trying to push its way out of me.

"Lee."

He cursed under his breath, wrapped one arm

around my shoulders, and squeezed my hand. "I've got you. I've always got you, Paige."

"My family's not going to be here," I whispered, my eyes filling with tears.

"Hey, I'm your family, too, remember?"

His voice was soft, and there were a thousand unanswered questions there, words that should have been said. But there was no time for that. Instead, I screamed into the pain, Lee taking the brunt of my anger, fear, and worry. The nurses were there suddenly, the fact that they were all goddesses in my eyes telling me that maybe I really should have found a way to get there earlier for the pain meds.

"I thought they said first births were supposed to take longer," I ground out, afraid that my parents and my family wasn't going to be there in time.

But Lee was there, holding me, and as the doctor told me to push, I did, even as fiery pain and determination slammed through me.

My sister had explained that I would forget some of the pain, terror, and fear because that was how people were able to have second babies and thirds. Because they forgot the awful agony of childbirth.

I didn't know if I would ever forget the anguish and guttural fear, but right now, all I could focus on was doing what the doctor said and squeezing Lee's hand. His gentle breathing and whispered, nonsensical words in my ear kept me steady. And when I was practically lying on him, he kissed the top of my head and held me close.

At the first sound of the baby's cry, overwhelming emotion slammed into me, and tears fell. Lee kissed my tears away as his eyes widened.

"Would you like to cut the cord, Lee?" the doctor asked. I blinked, looking up at him.

"You can," I whispered as the doctors continued to work.

"Are you sure? I mean..."

"It's okay," I cried.

And so he reached out, cut the cord, and I watched as Lee Grier, the hot, sexy, manly man who was my brother's best friend and *my* best friend, cried as he did so.

And then they put the baby on my chest, all wiggling limbs and a scrunched-up face of pure anger and outrage. I held her close and put her on my breast as the nurses continued wiping her down.

"Emery, happy birthday," I whispered.

"Happy birthday, baby," Lee mumbled right next to me as he held out his hand. Emery immediately tapped on his finger but didn't latch on. She was far too young for that, but she was touching him, and I saw the pure love in Lee's gaze.

And right then, I fell in love. Not once, but twice.

With the baby girl in my arms, with how she made me feel as if she were the only thing in the world.

I fell in love with my daughter.

But I also fell in love with the man now holding her as the nurse took care of me. With that, I knew what I had been feeling long before I had let myself believe it. I hadn't felt anything like this with Colton. No, that emotion had been a mere fade of what I felt for this man. And not because he was holding my daughter with such love and tenderness in his gaze and his touch. But because of the man he was.

The man I really had fallen in love with. Just like I knew right then and there, that he had fallen head over heels for my daughter. I didn't know what to say, and I was sure that saying anything right then would be too much.

After the nurses had cleaned Emery and me up, I held my daughter close as Lee brushed my hair, muttering little things to my baby as I rubbed her cheek with my finger.

I loved Lee, but I loved Emery, too.

And my child needed me. Frankly, I wanted Emery to need Lee, too. Because with that look, I knew he wouldn't walk away. And letting myself fall for him in the open, allowing myself to make the mistake of pushing him away would hurt my daughter.

So, I wouldn't. I would find a way for him to be in

Emery's life, but I wouldn't break him, and I wouldn't tie him to me.

Because Lee and Emery deserved better than that.

I was a mother, and I was a friend.

And maybe, just maybe, that would be enough.

CHAPTER 13

Lee

I smiled down at the photo on my screen and shook my head. Paige had sent a selfie of a happy-looking Emery lying on top of Paige's chest after lunchtime.

I shook my head and texted back.

Me: *Looking good. Our girl spit up in your hair yet today?*

I knew I was a little too territorial and protective when it came to her. With Emery, at least. I was trying not to be so with Paige. While I wasn't Emery's father, sometimes I felt I was as good as. I was getting good at the whole filling the uncle-role thing. And though Paige's father and brothers constantly helped out, I felt as if I had a special connection with Emery. After all, I had been there when she was born. Yes, the rest of the Montgomerys had shown up soon after Emery was born, and she and Paige had been cleaned up. But I had been the one who was there—no one else. And I felt like I had a special right to them, even if I knew it was stupid.

But Emery had taken a part of my heart, and I wasn't ever going to get it back. And, frankly, I didn't need it back. Not when I knew it'd be safe in that baby girl's palms.

Paige: *I don't want to talk about the amount of vomit I have on me right now. I'm going to set her down for a nap soon, and then I will be ready to shower. Oh my God, I cannot wait to shower.*

I laughed, remembering the last time that Emery had spit up down my back. Somehow, it had gotten beneath the collar, and vomit had been everywhere. For a baby less than ten pounds, a lot of projectiles sure came out of her.

Me: *I have a few meetings today, but I do plan on coming for dinner. Okay?*

Paige: *Can you bring diapers? How the hell do we already need more diapers? I thought Mom was just kidding* *when she said that I would need twelve times the number of diapers that I ever thought I would possibly need.*

I laughed. I couldn't help it.

Me: *What's funny is that you even told Annabelle when the twins came home that signing up for the diaper service was the best present you could give. And yet, here we are, needing more and more diapers.*

Paige: *Don't throw my words back in my face. I don't appreciate it.*

She sent a laughing emoji afterward, and I rolled my eyes.

Me: *Take care of my girl. I'll be over later.*

Paige: *We'll be waiting.*

Knowing that I didn't call going over to her house *home* was such an odd feeling. I was very careful not to do so. As if the moment I did, it would cross a line. But Paige and I were now past the point of no return. I hadn't meant to fall the way I had, or be in this position. One minute I was just trying to be the good guy to help out my friend, and the next, here I was, working my ass off so I could get things done and make it home to Paige and a baby who wasn't mine.

It didn't help that that asshole Colton hadn't even met her yet. Oh, he was on his way, would be here soon, and Colton *had* met his child over the screen, but it wasn't the same. I had been there. I had been the one to hold her. I was the one who made her stop crying when it was over.

I didn't stay the night. That wasn't fair to Paige or Emery. Because a line had been drawn. One we hadn't even meant to happen. I was there for dinners, I was there over the weekends, but I didn't stay the night. I didn't act with Paige the way I wanted.

We would need to have a talk soon, once Paige was able to get a full night's sleep, and Emery slept through the night. Because I wasn't sure what else we were supposed to do, or how I was supposed to feel.

Because I had fallen in love with Paige Montgomery, and I hadn't meant to. And yet, something needed to happen. I needed her to know. Or maybe I just needed to know where I stood so when I was the man on the side, watching as Paige maybe fell in love again, and someone else raised that little baby girl I adored, I'd find a way to be okay with it.

Because Paige had only been meant to be my friend. I hadn't meant for any of this to happen. I was only supposed to be there to hold her hair back when she threw up during the first dregs of pregnancy.

And then we'd leaned on each other, and here I was. In love with a single mom and a baby girl like she was my own.

It didn't matter that Colton was the biological father and he'd somehow be in that little girl's life, even if it was different than anyone had planned. I still wanted them both. And I would have to be okay if that didn't happen. Somehow.

"I'm not trying to be nosy, but is that a photo of Emery?" Andrea asked as she walked in, a smile on her face.

I grinned and handed over my phone. "Right after lunch."

"I swear, that baby makes my ovaries want another one." She paused. "Should I not have said that to you?"

I laughed, shaking my head. "With the number of things I've talked over with Paige recently, you're fine. Plus, it's just the two of us in my office right now. You're welcome to say that you want another kid after looking at Emery. She is the best baby."

Andrea rolled her eyes. "She's pretty great. You're doing a good thing with that kid."

"What do you mean?" I asked, an odd sensation filling my belly.

"You and Paige. You guys are a great couple. And you're taking care of Emery like she's yours. I love to see it. You look happy, Lee."

I swallowed hard and did my best to look casual. I was failing. "I'm not with Paige. Not like that. I'm just her friend. Her parents and her siblings are there often, and Emery's never left wanting. But Paige and I are just friends."

Even as I said it, the words felt hollow. Andrea met my gaze and nodded.

"Oh. I'm sorry."

"Anyway, there's a few more pictures of Emery if you scroll to the left."

Andrea looked at me then and smiled, though it didn't quite reach her eyes. Awkwardness settled in, but she smiled over Emery's photos before handing my phone back.

"Are you heading into the lab?"

I nodded, sliding my phone into my pocket. "I have a few hours more to go. I just wanted to get through a couple of emails first."

"Okay, let me know if you need anything."

"No problem."

She left, and I felt like I was an idiot. I had no idea what the fuck I was doing when it came to Paige, but something needed to be done. Or maybe nothing at all. Perhaps this would just work out. Because while I knew Paige didn't want Colton back—the man was fucking married to someone else—it still felt complicated and twisted.

I didn't know what Paige wanted because neither of us ever spoke of it. And that would have to change. Only I was afraid as soon as I said something, I'd lose her and Emery. And I wasn't sure I could stomach that.

I needed to fucking be a man and do something.

I shook my head and stood, knowing I needed to focus on the science and the lab. I could worry about my personal life, or lack thereof, later.

My office phone rang as I walked past the front of my desk, and I answered it. "Lee Grier."

Someone let out a breath on the other end of the line before the phone clicked, the person hanging up.

I frowned, setting the phone back in its cradle, wondering who the hell kept calling.

They never spoke, but I always heard breathing on the line.

It was weird and bothered me, but when I asked the tech support team about it, they'd said they weren't sure what was going on. I wasn't sure what I was supposed to do about it, or what I *should* do. Instead, I went back to work and focused on anything but Paige, phone calls, and the fact that as soon as I spoke to her about what I felt, I might lose her because she had far more important things to worry about than my psyche.

I would focus on what I was good at. Research, creating, and just using my brain. It was easier to focus on science and math than it was anything else in the world. At least, that's what I told myself when it came to Paige Montgomery.

I was so deep into my work, my phone alarm buzzed, startling me. I looked up, blinking.

I snorted, then turned off my alarm and headed out

of the office. The only way I could focus on getting out on time and making sure Paige and Emery were fed was if I set alarms for myself. I tended to work longer hours than I needed to because I enjoyed it. And yet, I had something to look forward to now. Some*one* to look forward to. Maybe.

My phone buzzed again, and I looked down.

Benjamin: *Are you heading to Paige's for dinner?*

I picked up my phone and called. "Hey, I'm heading out to my car now. I didn't want to text and fall. And, yeah, I was going to pick up some diapers and head over there, is that okay?"

"Sounds good to me. I just wanted to see in case I should go over."

I snorted. "You have a baby at home, too, you know."

"He's so big right now. I swear he's grown four sizes this month. I can't believe how quickly time goes by."

I laughed at that image. "Right? Are you bringing Rafael into Montgomery Builders now?"

"Yeah, this was the first week that we got it going. It's easier for me than Brenna. But it works."

"How's Brenna doing not being near Rafael every hour?"

"She stopped by the place four times today, and I'm out in the field. It's not like I get to see my kid every hour. I don't think I like this. I'm thinking about strapping him to my back at some point if I don't have to do too much manual labor. We'll see."

I smiled, picturing big, bad Benjamin Montgomery with a baby strapped to his body as he planted trees. "That could work."

"I'm thinking about it. We'll go over the logistics. I know Paige will have Emery in there, but at least she'll be next door to the nursery."

"You guys are a good family, and the fact that you can make a program work like that is great."

Benjamin laughed. "Our cousins did it first. And we're testing it out. However, I do like it."

"Good. I don't think that could work here." There was a pause, and I thought about what I'd said. "Not that I would bring Emery with me. Unless, you know, there was an emergency or something."

"We're all here for her, Lee. But we're glad that you're there for her, too."

"Um. Right."

"Do I want to know what you're doing with my sister?" Benjamin asked after a moment.

I got to my car and frowned, looking around. It felt like someone was watching me, but maybe it was just the fact that I was talking with Benjamin. I didn't know, but I pushed those thoughts away and got into my car, setting up the Bluetooth as I tried to force my thoughts into some semblance of order.

"I don't know, Ben. That's a problem, isn't it? I have no idea what the fuck's going on with your sister and me. And I probably shouldn't be the one to tell you that."

"No, you being as confused as we are helps." Benjamin let out a breath. "The only reason we gave her as much space as she wanted was because she asked for it. We're not assholes who force ourselves into being with her all the time. But you were there. And when you weren't, one of us was. We're never alone, we Montgomerys. But I just don't want either of you guys hurt. You know?"

"I know. Fuck, it's just…it's Paige."

"Yeah, it's Paige. You should tell her how you feel, bro."

I laughed, heading out of the parking lot. "Yes, just like you did with Brenna?"

"Worked out for me in the end."

"Maybe you took all the luck and I'll end up being that weird uncle-friend guy who shows up for some parties."

"You're still my best friend, Lee. No matter what happens."

"You really think that any of you would want me near Paige if it turned out that we didn't fit?"

"That's up to you. But I see how you are around her, the way you are around Emery. Don't let everything slip through your fingers because you're afraid. I know that whatever the two of you are doing is completely opposite of how a normal relationship should work. But hell, you two are practically an old married couple already. Maybe you should talk to each other."

"You're starting to sound more like Archer than yourself." I scowled.

"Pretty much. But my baby brother taught me a lot. We should listen to him."

"Maybe. Or perhaps we should just keep things how they are."

"As an amorphous blob that doesn't make any sense and makes everybody confused and wanting to step on eggshells so as not to hurt each other's feelings? Sure, that sounds great."

"I hate when you're the voice of reason."

My friend laughed. "You must hate me often, asshole."

I rolled my eyes, then hung up, finally heading towards the store. I picked up diapers and chocolate for Paige since she didn't let herself have it often, and then headed towards the house.

This wasn't what I wanted for my life. I had told myself that I wouldn't have this. That I wasn't going to rely on anyone or fall in love. Because my parents had been in love. They had moved around a lot, but had loved one another and had been there for each other.

And then biology changed everything, and it left my mother broken, tearing something open in me, too. I didn't want that. I didn't want that for Paige.

What if my genes flipped? How was I supposed to let someone trust me when I couldn't even trust my own biology? I frowned at that thought and then pulled into Paige's driveway before letting myself head inside.

Paige was in the kitchen, rocking Emery as she smiled over the baby's head. "You're here."

I couldn't help but smile back. "I am. And not too late, either."

"Eliza and Beckett brought over dinner. So, we don't have to cook."

My stomach growled as I nodded. "Nice."

"It's a broccoli chicken casserole bake thing. And I'm starving."

"I'm suddenly starving, too. You okay with me eating dinner with you?"

She blinked, and I realized that we hadn't spoken about me eating dinner over here. We had just assumed. And maybe this was the perfect time to talk about things.

I set down the diapers and the chocolate and then took Emery from Paige's arms. The baby looked up at me, her still-blue eyes wide, and I grinned. "There's my girl," I whispered. I looked up at Paige, and she blinked at me before a single tear ran down her cheek. "Hey, don't cry."

"I want to blame it on the hormones, but I don't think I can. You're just so good with her, Lee."

"Emery's an easy baby to love." I held out my free arm, and Paige slid into my side, holding me close. "We need to talk, Paige," I said after a moment, knowing that I was going to break this moment and change the way we were. But I had to. I couldn't *not* love this little girl and the woman in my arms, and I needed to be able to walk away if I was forced to. If I didn't, I would end up breaking all of us in the process.

Paige pulled away and then wiped her face. "I know. I'm just really not good at the talking part. At least when it comes to me. Anyone else, I can get them to tear open their hearts and pour their feelings into the conversation so I can figure out what's going on. And yet when it comes to me? Not so much. It just doesn't work out."

"Good. We're the same way. Except for the fact that I suck at communicating with anybody but about the most trivial things."

She rolled her eyes. "We both know that's not true."

"Well, recently, at least for the last nine months or so, I've been really good about not stepping over the line and talking about what's important."

Emery gurgled in my arms, and I rocked her,

looking down at the little baby that held my heart. "I don't think I can do this, Paige."

Paige let out a shocked breath, and I held back a curse. "I mean, I don't think I can hold this little girl, hold *you,* and not want more. This wasn't what I planned. I still don't know what the hell I'm doing."

"Don't curse in front of the baby," she said quickly, and we both laughed.

"You guys are Montgomerys. It's going to be hard not to curse. I'll try. But like I was saying, I know that we've been so good about trying to remain friends and not talking about the important things between us. And yet we have to. Don't we? We started to the day she was born, and then we pushed everything aside for obvious reasons. I don't think I can do that anymore."

Paige bit her lip and nodded. "I know. I know. I've been so selfish in wanting you in my life, and yet I also know that you have your own. You need to be able to do what you want."

"That's not what I'm saying," I whispered as Emery's eyelids began drooping. "I'm telling you that I want more, Paige. That I'm tired of pretending." Paige's eyes widened, and I shook my head. "You can't be surprised."

"I just thought that our one time was to relieve stress or tension. Ever since then, you've just been such a good friend. I haven't wanted to break things."

I sighed, wondering why it was so hard for me to

just tell her. "I know. We've both been good at dancing around the subject, and yet, here it was. We've spent more time together than I have with any of my previous girlfriends. I held you when you gave birth, Paige. There's no going back."

"I don't want to ruin this, Lee."

"Paige," I whispered, letting my heartbeat slow from its rapid pace for just an instant. "We've been more for a while. You know that."

She nodded, and then I leaned forward, over her baby girl, and kissed Paige softly. "We've been more. And maybe we should own up to it."

Paige leaned back and licked her lips. "So, nothing will change?"

"Some things might," I whispered, letting the hunger seep into my voice.

Paige's eyes widened, and then she smiled. "Oh, that. Some things. I think we've been so good about not talking about what this is, that I've confused myself. So maybe we should just try. As long as we don't hurt Emery or each other."

"Never. That's the number one rule. We let ourselves be who we are, what we've been without talking about it, but I can kiss you."

"You've been kissing me, Lee. That's part of the problem."

"Well, now I can kiss you and not confuse us both."

"You're saying this as if it's easy."

"Nothing with us is ever easy, Paige. But maybe we should try."

When I kissed her again, she didn't pull away. And when Emery cried between us, Paige took her back, fed her, and I heated up our dinner. Paige was right. Nothing had changed.

But *everything* had.

Everything had changed.

And I had to hope to hell that we hadn't just made a mistake that would cost us everything.

CHAPTER 14

Lee

"When was the last time we had a guys' night?" Beckett asked as he rubbed the back of his neck.

I looked up from my phone and frowned. "When were the twins born?" I teased.

Benjamin laughed. "At least Rafael is sleeping through the night."

"The twins, not so much," Jacob put in.

I shook my head. "Yeah, Emery doesn't know what sleep is, though I don't have to deal with that as Paige does."

The guys gave each other a look, and then each raised a brow at me.

"What?"

"So, we're not going to talk about the fact that you're with our sister, but maybe not, and we don't know what's going on?" Benjamin asked, resting his hands over his stomach.

"I would like to know what's going on," Archer put in as he popped a melon ball into his mouth.

"Yes, we all would," Jacob teased. "Seriously, tell us."

"Tell us," Marc added.

He leaned against Archer, the two of them sharing a look, and I shook my head. "We're just... I don't know. Should we be talking about something else?" I asked, my voice going slightly high-pitched.

"You're the one who brought up Paige and Emery," Beckett said, shaking his head. "It is all your fault."

"It's not what you think."

"Well, what *should* we think?" Archer asked, teasing.

"I don't know. Don't we think this is weird?" I asked, looking at my friends. "This is your sister we're talking about."

"And we trust you," Beckett hedged. "At least, we should, shouldn't we? We're not Neanderthals who are going to beat you up for daring to look at our sister. After all, you didn't leave her alone and pregnant and haven't even met the fucking baby yet." Beckett's voice lowered to a growl.

I wrapped my hand around my beer bottle and held back a growl of my own.

"I guess you're right on that. I want to murder him. He keeps trying to get out here, but work is in the way."

"Work," Archer repeated, using his fingers as air quotes.

"Why are we even letting him get a say?" Marc growled. "He shouldn't be allowed to. Not when he hasn't stepped up to his responsibilities. It shouldn't matter that he and Paige aren't together. He did the crime. Now, he has to do the time."

I looked at Marc, trying to figure out exactly what he meant by that. Thankfully, Jacob was the one who spoke, rather than one of Paige's brothers. "I hope you're not calling Emery a crime and fatherhood *time,* but I'm sure you just meant that he has to lean into his responsibilities and take care of what he fucking did."

Marc sighed. "Of course. I like Paige. She's sweet, organized, and always on time for things. She doesn't deserve to do all of this alone because she dated an asshole."

"And that's why I love you," Archer put in, leaning into his husband.

Marc smiled, his eyes lightening. "I'm just saying,

Colton deserves whatever he gets, but he doesn't deserve Paige."

I nodded tightly. "Damn straight."

"So, you're saying you're the one who deserves Paige, then?" Archer asked sweetly.

I sighed and set down my beer as I wasn't in the mood to drink anyway. "I don't know what's happening, but I am taking Paige out on a date tomorrow. With Emery. The three of us. A date."

Beckett and Benjamin gave each other a look and clinked beer bottles in cheers. While Jacob just looked smug.

"It's about time." Archer clapped his hands, while Marc rolled his eyes.

"Seriously, you all don't care?" I asked, confused as to where this conversation was going.

"All we're saying is that you have been practically dating our sister for nearly a year anyway. You're a good guy. We like you. And you're our friend. If we didn't like you, and if you weren't good enough for Paige, we wouldn't be hanging out with you. Not that we could ever tell Paige what to do. She's her own person and would likely kill us if we tried to tell her what to do." Beckett nodded.

"Plus, there's the whole castration thing that the girls seem to love," Jacob added, and we all visibly shuddered.

"Can we please change that? I don't want to teach Emery that castration is the way to go."

"Look at you, thinking that you're going to be teaching Emery in the long term," Archer joked, a broad smile on his face.

Marc shushed him. "I think you can clearly see that Lee is out of his depths here. This is the guy who promised he would never date seriously, and suddenly, he's dating a woman with a baby, a baby that he helped bring into the world. It changes things. Let's be nice."

Never in my life would I have thought I would agree with Marc, let alone be thanking him and being on his side. Clearly, I had lost my damn mind. Not that Marc was a bad person, I just never understood him or really hung out with him enough to have these kinds of moments.

"The problem is, we couldn't do anything when it came to Colton," Benjamin said after a moment. "Not that we would. But we protect our sister at all costs, and at some point, we have to realize that she is an adult who makes her own decisions. Stepping in would only hurt her or piss her off. So, we're there when she needs us to lean on, but we don't force boyfriends out of her life."

"That's good," I began, wondering what I should say.

"Of course, we always growl and try to intimidate the guys, but they never seem to go away." Beckett glared at Marc and Jacob, who just grinned and shook their heads.

"Sorry, I'm not going anywhere," Jacob teased while Marc leaned into Archer, a small smile playing on his face

"When Paige told us she was pregnant, we might've freaked out a bit. But, mostly, we hated the way Colton treated her," Archer added.

"I hate him," I growled.

"Because of the way he treated Paige? Or because you think that he stands in the way of what you could have?" Benjamin asked softly, and I flinched, the question hitting home a little too hard.

Archer leaned forward and patted my knee. "Colton will never be the problem. It will always be what you and Paige decide that works between you. Remember that."

I looked at Archer after he spoke and swallowed hard. "She's been hurt so much. I don't want to be the guy who hurts her again."

"Then don't be," Jacob added. "Because, honestly, we stayed away from Colton because we didn't want to hurt Paige or the pregnancy. But if you hurt her, you're our best friend. We *will* kill you."

I laughed with the others, even though I felt like maybe they weren't joking. Though I would probably deserve it.

The doorbell rang at that point, and I frowned, looking at the group of men there.

"Did Clay and Riggs say they were coming?

"No, Storm and Everly have the kids, so they have a date tonight. They're probably screwing like bunnies and enjoying the time off," Archer added while Marc just sighed.

"Really?" Archer's husband muttered.

"I'm just saying. It's the truth."

I got up, ignoring the guys muttering and joking behind me. I walked to my front door and opened it, confused at the lack of anyone there. "Is somebody dinging and ditching? Is that still a thing?" Then I looked down and saw the wilted roses and the note, and my blood froze in my veins.

"What is it?" Jacob asked from behind me.

I couldn't believe this was happening. We weren't at my office anymore. No, this person, whoever it was, knew where I lived. I knew the look of that note; the feel of it near me. Unless I had two people sending me weird things like this, things had just escalated.

"I think I have a stalker," I whispered.

"Are you serious? What the hell is that?" Jacob snarled, the anger in his voice reminding me that Annabelle had once had a stalker, too. I hadn't been there to help either of them when everything went to hell, but I'd seen the aftermath. I didn't want to think that this was in the same realm as what had happened with the two of them, but I just didn't know anymore.

"What the fuck am I supposed to do?" I ran my hand through my hair, staring out into the distance as if the darkness held answers instead of more questions.

Benjamin moved closer, hovering over my shoulder. He was a couple of inches taller than me, and I had a feeling he wanted to push me out of the way to see what was happening. "Why do you think you have a stalker?"

I turned to him, shaking my head as I tried to process everything. I wanted to scream, run after whoever the hell was doing this. When it came to work, I was better at working through problems with my mind. Yet right now, all I wanted to do was use my fists. But I didn't think that was an option here—not with the unknown pressing in so tightly, I knew I could suffocate. Finally, I took a deep breath and answered. "Because there are wilting, dead roses with a note, and this isn't the first one I've gotten."

"Why is this the first time we're hearing about it?" Beckett asked.

"Because I didn't put two and two together, and it's been nearly a year. I didn't think anything of it at first because I thought it was a joke by one of my friends from college. But it wasn't him, and it wasn't frequent enough for anything to really make sense or come together." I let out a breath. "What do I do?"

Benjamin pulled me into the house. "We're calling the cops, we're taking some photos, and you're going to tell us everything."

I swallowed hard. "Do I tell Paige?" I asked softly.

"Depends on if you want to start your relationship on a lie or not?" Archer asked. "Let's see what happens tonight, but you should tell her."

I nodded, looked at the guys, and then pulled out my phone. "Fuck," I muttered.

"Who do you think it is?" Beckett asked as he shut the door and locked it.

"I have no clue." I ran my hand over the back of my neck. "I've been trying to think about who it could be for months now, and it doesn't make any sense. Like I said, I thought it was that friend from college, then maybe one of you for a second until I realized it didn't seem like a Montgomery thing. *Then* I thought it could be a competitor, but that didn't make any sense, either. None of this makes any fucking sense."

"You have had a few ex-girlfriends in the past," Benjamin added.

I scowled. "Just because I've slept with a few women doesn't mean that I dated women who would stalk me."

My best friend sighed and squeezed my shoulder.

"Maybe not, but let's go through everyone anyway. The cops are going to ask these questions, too."

I cursed under my breath but went through the motions. The authorities came and took my statement but without the other notes in hand, and given the odd timing, there really wasn't much they could do. I'd at least done something, but it didn't feel like enough.

All I could hope for was that this would go away, and no one would get hurt, and yet I didn't know if that was even possible. Not with the escalation, and not with the eerie feeling that wouldn't quite fade.

The night became oddly subdued and ended quickly after that. I got into bed, smiled at the photo Paige had sent me of Emery, and told myself that I was overreacting. Only those dead flowers, the red roses like a stain against the white concrete of my front porch, told me that maybe I wasn't overreacting.

THE NEXT EVENING, I told myself that everything would be fine and that I needed to focus on the here and now—even if I didn't quite believe that.

"Ready to go?" I asked as I stood in the doorway, watching Paige set Emery up in her car seat.

"I think so," Paige answered, looking over the diaper bag. "Are you sure it's okay that we're bringing Emery with us?"

I smiled and moved forward, running my hand down her back. Paige turned to me, her mouth parted slightly. I wanted to lean down and kiss those swollen lips, but I refrained, only because I knew it would be hard to stop once we began.

"I'm not going to force you to leave Emery home for a night out when she's so small. We'll go to our favorite place, and they know we're coming in. Meaning, they are prepped for us. We'll get a table away from everyone else, and she'll be covered. If she starts crying, one of us can pick her up, and we'll come home. We're just going to try it out. If it doesn't work, then we can try something different."

Paige smiled, though worry still filled her gaze. "If you're sure. I know Annabelle or any of my other siblings or my parents could take Emery, but then I'd have to leave her with them, and we both know that's just not going to happen." She laughed as she said it, even though it was the truth—one I completely felt deep in my soul.

I smiled and kissed Paige softly, needing her taste. Tonight felt weird, and yet it wasn't. It was as if we had just fallen into these roles, and yet we were traversing something far different than usual. This was us trying to figure out if we could make this work beyond pretending that we weren't who we were. It would get complicated. Then again, everything we had done recently was complicated.

"I know. I don't want to leave Emery behind, either. So, we won't. We'll take her out, and if this doesn't work, then I'll make you something fancy here."

"Our *something fancy* is like tuna casserole, Lee."

"If I bake it and add cheese and breadcrumbs to it, it's practically gourmet."

She snorted, and I leaned forward and plucked Emery's car seat off the kitchen island. She was already passed out, all tucked into her little blanket like a burrito, looking comfortable and adorable.

Paige leaned into me as she looked at Emery. "I pumped just in case we need to feed her during dinner, and I didn't feel like whipping out my boob in the middle of our meal."

My gaze went to her chest, her very nice and voluptuous chest, considering she was breastfeeding.

She narrowed her eyes at me. "You're thinking about my tits right now, aren't you?"

"I really can't help it. Your boobs are fantastic."

She swallowed hard. "We can't have sex yet," she blurted.

I raised my brows, nodding. "I read the books. I know. Plus, I kind of like that we've been taking this slow."

Paige snorted. "We had sex before we even decided to date, Lee. How is that taking it slow?"

"Because we've had months of pretending we weren't dating when we were?"

She bit her lip, and I wanted to lean forward and kiss away the sting. Only the fact that Emery was between us in the car seat held me back. "We have been, haven't we?"

"I haven't been with anyone else. Not since before you and I slept together. No dates, not since that night in the rain."

She looked at me then, her eyes wide. "I was always afraid to ask."

"You shouldn't have been. It's just me. I promise. I don't know what's going to happen next, but you're stuck with me."

"I wouldn't mind being stuck with you."

"It's pretty sweet." I leaned forward and kissed her again because I couldn't help it, and then we made our way to my SUV. We had bought the set of car seats where it had two bases. I had one base in my vehicle, and she had one in hers. As if we were already playing at being a family before we decided to call it what it was.

This was probably a fucking mistake, but I didn't mind. I wanted to know if this could work. If we weren't just placating ourselves.

We made our way to the restaurant, speaking mostly of Emery's big day. "I swear she's going to be able to roll over any day."

"At three weeks?" Paige asked, laughing. "Seriously?"

"Seriously. She's so brilliant."

"I mean, I believe she's brilliant, and I know she is. However, she's not going to start walking any day now. Stop making my baby grow up before I've even had a chance to have her."

"I promise I won't do that."

Paige laughed, and I loved the sound of it filling the car. "That's what you say. But why do I feel like she's already going off to college?"

"This is going to be an interesting eighteen years if you're already worried about that."

She just snorted. "Always going to worry."

"Well, I'm here. I've got you." I kissed the back of her hand, and she pressed her lips together, smiling as we pulled into the parking lot. I helped her get Emery out of the car, doing my best not to watch her curves sway as she did. Paige was seriously distracting in the best ways possible.

I held Emery's car seat, and Paige held the diaper bag, and when our familiar hostess waved at us, she beamed. "I heard you were bringing in the baby. I'm so excited. We got you your normal table, and since it's a weeknight, we should be able to give you as much privacy as possible. That way, everybody doesn't come and try to meet the baby. But, oh my gosh, she's adorable—beautiful, Paige."

"Thank you. She's the light of my life."

"She's looking good." Carla looked between us and beamed. "Are you going to tell us if this is a date or not? Or are you two just going to keep telling us you're friends?"

"Carla," I warned, and she waved us off.

"No worries. I'll get you to your table. I'd say a glass of champagne is on the house, but...are you drinking?"

Paige shook her head. "Not yet. Emery's feeding schedule's a little too tight right now for that to work. Plus, you know, I'd fall asleep after one glass."

"No problem. Sparkling cider it is. Congratulations, Mom." Carla squeezed Paige's hand, and I watched as Paige's eyes watered a bit.

"Fricking hormones," she muttered, and we both took our seats, setting Emery up between us. The baby kept sleeping, and we covered her up a bit to shield her from the bright lights. "She looks comfortable. But I still feel like maybe we should have stayed at home."

"We can leave," I added.

"No. We're adults. We've got this. I know it's early, but we're in a decent situation where we're in charge of as many outcomes as possible. We can make this work."

"Sounds good to me."

"Hello, I'm Jordan, and I'll be taking care of you tonight," an unfamiliar woman's voice said from beside us.

"Hello, Jordan," I said, smiling back.

She grinned. "Oh, look. I love when Mom and Dad get to come out for a date night. Now, if you'll just bear with me, this is only my second night here, and I'm still getting used to the menu."

I froze at the words *Mom* and *Dad,* but Paige just kept smiling, though I saw the look of panic flash in her eyes. Carla knew us from before, so it hadn't been weird. But this person didn't. I mean, everyone who saw us together would naturally think we were a family. A real one. And I wasn't quite sure what I was supposed to do with that or how to make sure that Paige knew I wasn't going to rush her. Hell, I was still getting used to the whole thing myself.

Paige just smiled and took our drink orders. When Carla came by with the sparkling cider, she whispered fiercely under her breath, "We're so sorry. I forgot that this was Jordan's section for the night. She didn't mean anything by it."

"Don't worry about it," Paige said. "Most of the people at the birthing classes were very confused when we had to explain that he's not the daddy."

I grimaced. "Other people thought I must have been one of her two thousand brothers."

"I can totally see that happening. However, I am kind of sad that you're now off the market, Lee," Carla added with a wink.

"Oh?" Paige asked, her voice brittle. Carla just rolled her eyes. "I'm just saying. Now all of the Montgomerys and their best friends are taken. Though I know you guys are just dating, so I'm not going to barge in with craziness. However, I'm kind of sad that all of your brothers went off and got married like all at the same time. I never had a chance." She sighed as she said it, and I laughed, knowing what Carla was getting at.

Paige snorted. "The number of women who come after my brothers still, even though they're married, is ridiculous."

Carla's eyes widened. "Are you serious? If I ever see that happening when they're on a date here, I'll tell them what's what. You don't mess with the Montgomerys or their families. And I'd like to think I'm an honorary Montgomery with the number of times I've fed all of you."

I grinned as Carla walked away and shook my head. "You know, I like her."

Paige raised a brow. "How much do you like her?" she teased.

"I never dated her if that's what you're worried about."

"I wasn't worried at all, but you would have been welcome to date her before."

I frowned. "I've dated a few people in my life, Paige."

"Don't remind me," she ground out, even though she was still smiling.

"As I was saying, I've dated a few people before, but I was always monogamous. And I'd like to think I'm not the asshole who just leaves women in my wake."

Paige shook her head, her gaze warming. "I know you aren't, Lee. Why do you think I'm out with you right now with my daughter? She's the most important thing in my life, but we're here. I mean, it's weird as hell that the waitress thought we were already a family. And here we are, on our first date, even if we might have been somewhat dating before. This is our first real date, Lee. And it's with a baby. Nothing we're doing is normal or according to any dating handbook out there."

"Since when do we need a handbook when it comes to dating?"

Paige bit her lip. "Because I'm not good at it. As evidenced by my exes."

"I'm not good at it, either. You know that. You know I didn't plan on anything serious." Her eyes shuttered, and I held back a curse at my words. "This is serious, Paige. I wouldn't risk our friendship, I wouldn't risk my relationship with your brothers, and I sure as hell wouldn't risk Emery for anything less than serious." It scared me that I was putting so much on the line, but I couldn't help it. She needed to know.

"I know, Lee. I know."

As Jordan came back to take our order, I smiled at the woman in front of me and had to tell myself that we were taking this seriously. Yes, we were risking everything, but it had to be worth it, because this was Paige.

And I didn't want to go anywhere.

CHAPTER 15

Paige

"Why am I so nervous?" I asked as I rocked Emery in my arms. She looked so cute in her dove-gray onesie with her little bow mouth puckered. She smiled up at me, or at least I thought it was a smile. It was probably gas. Could babies smile at a month old? I wasn't sure anymore since all the baby books had blended into my mind at this point, and all I could think about was the fact that Colton was on his way to the house.

"I don't know why you *wouldn't* be nervous," Archer said as he leaned forward and ran the back of his knuckle along Emery's cheek. "This is the first time Colton is seeing her in person. After such a weird-ass year, I would be a little freaked out, too."

"That somehow helped me. I don't know if it was supposed to help me, but it did."

My brother smiled at me, then leaned forward and kissed my forehead. "You're going to be fine. It's hard not to fall in love with this little pumpkin right here." He grinned down at my daughter, and I held back a happy sigh.

"She is pretty amazing. Perfect in every way."

"Oh, good, you've caught the same bug that Annabelle and Brenna got with their kids."

I knew he was teasing, but I wanted to nip that argument in the bud since my sisters and I were all on the same page. "I know that she's not perfect, and nobody ever will be since perfection doesn't exist. Trying to attain that only leads to stress. However, right now, looking this cute? That's my idea of perfection."

"Good answer, Mom," Archer teased. "Do you want me to be here?"

"No, I need to do this alone. Although Tarryn will be here, too," I gritted out.

"Dear God, that's right. She's Emery's stepmom." Archer's eyes widened. "Why didn't I put that together?"

"I find it hard to wrap my mind around, too. This

woman, however nice she may seem through video calls, is somehow connected to my daughter. But I can't be selfish. This will be good for Emery. The more people who love her and take care of her and want to be purposeful and important parts of her life, the better."

"That's a very healthy way to think about it. I'm proud of you."

"I also want to scratch the woman's eyes out, but I feel like that's on me."

Archer snorted and then hugged me tightly. "I'm going to head out before they get here. But I'm only a phone call away if you need me. As is Lee."

I heard the tone in my brother's voice and did my best to ignore it. "He has an important presentation today. I don't want to bug him."

"You *should* bug him. He's your boyfriend. And Emery is very important to him. You know the only reason he isn't here is that you practically pushed him out of the house."

"I did what I had to do to make sure he didn't get in the middle of it. Because I don't want him to feel like he needs to hurt Colton for merely existing."

"Existing and not existing close enough to be a father," Archer grumbled.

"I'm trying to be a better person. Let that happen."

"Whatever you say." Archer kissed my cheek again

and then headed out after saying sweet goodbyes to Emery.

That left me alone in my living room, holding Emery close and wondering if I was doing the right thing.

Colton hadn't been able to make it out to Colorado because of work, and he hated it. I hated it, too. Because while part of me had loved Colton, the other part couldn't be allowed to resent him for not being here. That would somehow hurt Emery, and I didn't want that to happen. He had given me Emery. I couldn't hate him for that. Only I wasn't sure what I was supposed to do now.

Because the one person I wanted to be here, the guy I wanted to be a part of this, couldn't be. At least not today. Because I couldn't let Lee be in the same room with Colton without Lee probably punching the other man. I knew Lee that well. Hell, I loved him.

I wasn't supposed to love him. He was only supposed to be my friend through all of this, yet somehow, we had become something more to each other, and I was so afraid that I would rely on that so much that he would leave.

After all, Colton had left.

I frowned and pushed those thoughts from my mind, focusing on Emery in my arms.

"Okay, baby girl. Time to meet your daddy."

The words felt foreign on my tongue. Somehow, part of me pictured Lee in that role, and he practically *had* been. He had been there when Emery was born. Had changed more diapers than anyone else in my family other than me, and had held Emery when she got fussy. Emery fell asleep in his arms more than she did in mine, and I couldn't be jealous of that. Because Emery loved Lee just like Lee loved my baby girl.

Now, she would be meeting the other man in her life.

I just had to hope today would go okay.

The doorbell rang before I could let myself fall down another rabbit hole, and for that, I was grateful. I rolled my shoulders back and made my way to the next change in my life. When I opened the door, Colton stood there, his hair pushed back from his face, a little messy as if he'd run his hands through it a few times. He had an odd expression on his face as if he weren't sure why he was here or even how he had gotten here. Of course, that could just be Colton's normal expression. He was like that sometimes. A woman with glorious strawberry-blonde hair and natural, soft waves stood by his side. She looked like an Amazon, tall and in wedged heels, a small smile on her face. She wore a light dress that accentuated her curves. She was stunning, as was the emerald-cut ring on her finger and the matching wedding band. Colton wore khakis, a button-down shirt, and a matching wedding band. They looked like models from the coast, ready to jump out into the surf or maybe head out on a night on the town. They looked like they fit together—and maybe they did.

Because Colton wasn't mine, he was Tarryn's.

And I was okay with that.

"You're here," I said quickly as I moved back. Tarryn took the first step, pulling Colton in, and I held back a frown at that.

"Hi," Colton said, his gaze on Emery's, not mine. I didn't blame him. Emery was why he was here and why I was even letting him in my home.

We had created her together, and now, they were finally meeting.

"Emery Jillian Montgomery, meet your daddy. This is Colton."

Colton met my gaze for a minute, though I knew Emery's full name wouldn't be a surprise to him. I had known that she would be taking my name as I had full custody and the Montgomery name was important to my family. Colton hadn't said anything about it, had just agreed quietly. So quietly. It was a little unnerving.

He looked down at the baby in my arms, then back up at me. "She's so small. I mean, she looks small on video, but she's like smaller in person."

I smiled, holding back a shake of my head. He sounded the same as ever, and yet I felt nothing for him. That was progress, I supposed. "Yes. Though she's grown quite a bit in the past month."

"She's beautiful," Tarryn put in, and I turned to the other woman.

"I'm sorry. Hello, I'm Paige. And this is Emery. My daughter." We'd met online, but this moment felt far more awkward than I thought possible.

Tarryn smile widened. "It's so good to meet you in person. I know we did so over video, and it's awkward, but thank you for letting me into your home."

"You're Colton's wife. Of course, I'm going to let you into my home. I swear, everything's going to be okay. I'm not bitter or anything." I hadn't meant to say that last part, but Tarryn laughed, her face lighting up.

She was impossibly gorgeous, while I had merely done myself up decently with maternity jeans and a long-sleeve cotton shirt over a tank top. I had washed my hair that morning, though I hadn't blown it out since I hadn't had time. Emery had spit up everywhere, so I'd had to change my top, and my hair was still in slightly frizzy waves because of it, but it was fine. I looked okay. I had makeup on, at least a dab of it, and I counted that as a win.

Emery looked adorable, and so long as she didn't throw up on herself again, we would be okay.

"Would you like to hold her?" I asked Colton, and he

stood frozen for a moment before Tarryn reached out and gripped his arm.

"Colton," she whispered.

My ex met her gaze and nodded tightly. "Sure."

He held out his hands awkwardly, and I ignored the little clutch in my heart as I handed over our daughter and gently told him how to keep her head safe and to support her neck. He held her awkwardly, like a football he was afraid to drop, and looked down at her, his eyes wide. "Oh, wow," he sputtered. Tarryn looked at him then, and she bit her lip. But she didn't reach out to touch Emery. She didn't help Colton in any way. Instead, she just stood back as if she weren't sure what to do. Or maybe I was the one who didn't know what to do.

"She's still small for her percentile, but eating well, and has slept through the night twice now. She also loves to throw up. Even with burping, she loves it." I was rambling, and I couldn't help it. What was I supposed to say to the man who had donated half of Emery's genes but hadn't been there for anything else? I'd tried to keep him filled in on the past month's-worth of milestones, but I wasn't sure what was too much for him. Or not enough. It wasn't as though Colton had let me in on what he was thinking. He never had, and that was part of our problem.

"Is your family helping you?" he asked, and I

nodded. He wasn't looking at Emery but at me, and I tried to smile.

"My parents have been amazing, as have my siblings. Emery is never alone. Neither am I."

I didn't bring up Lee, and I didn't know why since Lee had been in the house during those video calls with Colton. Maybe it just felt odd to bring up another man, even though Colton had brought his wife today. Or maybe it was that I didn't want to tarnish Lee at all by making him feel like a replacement. Because from what I saw here, Colton looked like the one out of place. I wasn't sure *what* I was supposed to say.

Emery kicked then and then started to cry. Colton's eyes widened, and I quickly took Emery from his arms and rocked her. "I just need to set her down for a nap. I'm sorry. She sleeps more often than not."

He cleared his throat. "Oh, it's fine. I wanted to talk to you anyway."

Slightly unnerved, I rocked Emery back to sleep, then set her in her bassinet. "She'll still be in the room, but she just got a little fussy."

"Understandable," Colton said stiffly before looking at Tarryn.

I didn't know what was going on, and I wasn't sure what to think.

"I'm going to give you two some privacy. I have a couple of phone calls to make anyway. It was lovely to meet you, Paige." Tarryn walked out of the house then, confusing me.

I stiffened, worried. "What's wrong, Colton?"

He let out a breath, then looked at his hands. "You're doing a great job with Emery. I'm sorry that I left you in the lurch like this. I didn't mean to. I honestly thought that you'd be good out here with your family and your support system. I didn't realize that you were pregnant when I left."

I frowned. "I know you didn't. I didn't know I was pregnant until you were gone. I loved you, Colton," I said after a moment, and he blanched. "I know you didn't love me. And that's fine."

"Paige," he began, and I interrupted.

"You didn't love me enough, or maybe you didn't love me at all. I get that. We were in two different parts of the relationship, and I wasn't aware enough to understand that. Maybe I didn't love you enough to see it. But you brought Emery into my world, so I can never hate you. I can never resent you. Because I love that little girl so much. And without you, I wouldn't have her."

"I can't move back, Paige," he whispered, and I nodded.

I'd been ready for him to say that and hadn't expected anything else, honestly. "I know. It's okay. You don't need to move back here. It's fine. We'll make it work. You were able to come out here this weekend, after all. And you're right. I do have a support system. But Emery will always know that you are her father and that you love her."

Only he hadn't said those words. He hadn't said he loved me. Cold washed over me as he gave me a look, his eyes filled with remorse, and I wanted to scream. Only I didn't. I couldn't do anything in that moment.

He met my gaze fully, and I went cold. "I thought I was starting over, Paige. I love my wife. I love my life. And Tarryn and I? Kids aren't in our plans. I thought you understood that."

"Understood what?" I bit out, fisting my hands in front of me.

"I mean, we always used condoms, Paige. You were on birth control."

I would *not* hit him. It wouldn't help anyone. "Clearly, that didn't work. And we didn't always use a condom, Colton. Because I was on birth control, and both of us were clean."

"I realize that. And you are doing great with Emery. But…I never wanted to be a dad, Paige. I'm not good at it. My dad wasn't good at it. And, honestly, you're doing such a great job out here. And I think you should continue doing that."

I felt like he had slapped me and tried not to scream or react. "You want to sign over rights." He hadn't said the words, but I knew what he was getting at. At least one of us should be brave enough to say them.

He nodded, and I broke. Not for me, but for the little girl he'd never know. "I'm sorry. But you're so good at being a mom. And you have Lee." My eyes must have widened, and he shook his head. "I've seen the pictures. The ones that you send. I know Lee's hands. I know how you smile whenever you talk about him. He has been there for you and Emery. I get that. And I'm not that guy. I wish I was. But I'm not."

"You're going to walk out of her life." It wasn't a question. It didn't need to be. "You're going to walk away from your daughter and never look back. You could do that?"

I felt as if he'd just ripped something from me. Not a part of myself, but that connection. The part that I had thought I knew, the one where he would always take care of what was his. That his love for Emery would surpass anything. Did he not love her? How could he not?

I moved so I stood in front of the bassinet, blocking his view of Emery. I couldn't believe that she was in the room for this, and I was grateful that she was too young to understand any of it.

"I'm sorry. I'm just not that guy."

"Leave," I said, rolling my shoulders back. I didn't know where the strength came from, how the steel emerged. But I had to do this. Not for myself, but for Emery. I did not have another choice. "Go. I will have my lawyer send you the papers shortly. Thank you for saying it to my face. Now, leave."

"I'm sorry, Paige."

"I'm sure you will be." There wasn't anything to say after that. Colton left, and the car sped away with Tarryn behind the wheel.

I couldn't focus, couldn't breathe. Instead, I picked up Emery and held her close, trying not to break down.

When the door opened behind me, I sagged slightly. Whoever it was had a key, and I hoped to hell it was Lee. I turned and let out a relieved breath as he stood there, but he wasn't alone. Archer, Benjamin, and Beckett all stood with him, scowls on their faces.

"What happened?" Lee asked as he came forward. He wrapped his arms around me, kissed me softly, and took Emery from my hold. And just like that, I knew. I knew that no matter what happened, he was Emery's father. Even if Lee and I didn't work out, even if he broke my heart and we never spoke to each other again, he wouldn't leave Emery, because Lee wasn't that guy. A man who left and broke a little girl's heart. Yes, he could break mine. It could still happen. He could figure out that I was too much work or only want to be my friend, and I would take that. I would breathe through the pain because he wouldn't leave Emery. And that was the one thing I knew. The one thing that gave me hope.

"He left," I whispered as the tears threatened. I told them what had happened.

Beckett cursed under his breath and hugged me tightly. Benjamin took Emery from Lee's hold and walked her, waving her little fist in the air as she made noises in his arms. I was okay. I had to be okay.

Archer took Emery from Benjamin as my brother scowled at him, and Archer began to rock her, and then Beckett let go of me and took Emery, and Lee was holding me.

Suddenly, Emery was in my arms, and my brothers and Lee were holding me tightly, the four of them surrounding me.

"I don't want to hurt Emery's little ears by saying what I truly feel," Beckett began. "However, good riddance."

His eyes sparked, and I nodded tightly. "I've got you. I've got the girls. I've got my folks. I've got all of you." I met Lee's gaze, and he leaned forward and kissed me softly.

None of my brothers said a thing, and I was glad for it. "I'm here. Promise," Lee whispered.

I knew that because I wasn't alone. And I would do whatever I could with the power running through my veins to make sure Emery knew she was wanted. That everyone in her life was there because they loved her and wanted to be there for her. And when I leaned into Lee's hold, and Beckett and Benjamin gave each other a look as Archer smirked at me, I rolled my eyes. Lee flipped them off, and I laughed, surprising myself.

This wasn't how the day was supposed to go, but maybe, just maybe, we'd find a way to make it work.

CHAPTER 16

Lee

"Still no word on the note writer?" Benjamin asked as he helped me lift the box containing my new grill.

I adjusted my grip on the box and sighed. "Nothing at all."

"Does that worry you?" he asked.

"Yes, because I don't know what the fuck was going on before, and I still don't. However, we've had so many other things to worry about that I haven't focused on that since the last card."

"And you still haven't told Paige."

I cringed. "Every time I open my mouth to tell her, Emery spits up. Or something else happens. Like a certain asshole giving up rights to his kid."

"That man is lucky that I promised Paige I would not fly out there and kill him."

"Rafael wouldn't appreciate you dying or ending up in jail."

Benjamin scowled. "Are you saying I can't take Colton?"

"Shut up," I said with a laugh, thankful my best friend could find humor in the situation.

My friend sobered. "You need to tell her."

"I will." I let out a breath. "Even if nothing comes from the investigation and notes, I will tell her. I just want tonight to go well."

"You need to tell her tonight anyway."

"You're right, damn it. I need to. Because she's going to find out, even if we don't mean to keep secrets, we are. There goes the good date for the night."

Benjamin shook his head. "Being truthful with the woman that you're with isn't a bad thing."

I scowled. "I know. She's just had so much to worry about. I don't want to add something that hasn't been an issue for the past few weeks."

"It'll keep her and Emery safe if you do."

My blood ran cold, and I nodded tightly, reality setting in. "You're right. Fuck. Because whoever it is figured out where I live. They're bound to figure out where I'm at most days."

"If my sister gets hurt, I'm going to be the one who kills you because I can't get to Colton."

I nodded tightly. "If Paige gets hurt for me, I will gladly let you do it."

Benjamin met my gaze and shook his head. "Well, fuck. You make it hard to hate you."

"I hope so."

We finished putting together the grill, and Benjamin headed back to the house to be with Brenna and Rafael. Brenna's parents were in town to visit the baby, and they had wanted grandparent time. While Brenna worked on an order, Benjamin had been able to take some time to help me. I could have done it myself, but it was nice to hang out with my friend.

I looked around my modest home and figured that I'd done pretty well for myself, considering I'd started from nothing. After losing my parents, it had been touch and go for a while. Now, I owned this place, had some student debt, but not massive thanks to scholarships and grants, and was making do. Paige's house was bigger and Montgomery-made, though, and I liked it more. I tried not to think about what would happen if we went a step further because I couldn't see Emery growing up here. Not with the small backyard and not enough space. I would be there. Living with them.

I froze, wondering if that was going too far. Only, was it? We spent as much time together as possible. I loved that little girl. And I loved Paige. Not that either of us was ready for me to say that. We were going on our fourth date, and while she'd gotten the okay last week to have sex, we hadn't slept together yet because we were taking our time—or at least as much as we could.

And yet tonight, it felt different. Emery would be with Annabelle while she and Jacob took care of the twins and her. And then later, we would pick her up because there was no way we wanted to spend the night without Emery. Or at least, Paige didn't. It was still up in the air if I would be spending the night.

Hell, I wasn't sure I was good at this. I hadn't wanted a future and a forever, but here I was, thinking about it. With Paige. I knew I was probably moving too quickly, but hell, this wasn't what I had planned. Nothing was. Maybe that was a good thing.

I shook myself out of my thoughts, quickly showered, and got ready to pick up Paige. I put on dark gray pants and a black button-down shirt. I wasn't going to wear a tie or anything, but I thought I looked decent. I slung on a belt, put on some shoes, and brushed my hair back. It was getting a little too long, and I needed to cut it. But I also knew that Paige liked running her hands through it when we watched a movie. I would lay on her lap, with Emery sleeping on my stomach, and she'd either run her hands through my hair, or we'd hold hands over Emery's diapered bottom. Like we were a family.

Paige and Emery weren't anything I'd expected, but they were what I had. And I would do whatever I could to keep them.

Because Colton had thrown them away. And while part of me would always hate him, maybe I could be grateful at the same time because it had given me a chance. And that thought made me feel like a horrible person.

I grabbed my phone, wallet, and keys, and looked around the place, figuring it looked nice. Or at least, clean. I didn't know if we were coming back to my place or Paige's after dinner. I wasn't sure what the plans were. But I'd tried not to make my house look like I was a bachelor living alone, even though I only spent the night here. Most of my time was spent at work, with the Montgomerys, or with Paige.

When I pulled into Paige's driveway, I couldn't help but grin. She stood on the porch, dressed in a dove-gray wrap-around dress, her hair pulled back in a little updo, and she wore sexy-ass shoes that made me think about her legs wrapped around my shoulders as I ate her out, her heels digging into my back. I quickly quashed that thought, adjusted myself in my pants, and made my way out of the car.

"I think we match," I teased, and she looked between us and blushed. "I think dressing Emery in so many cute little gray outfits with dots of color has rubbed off on me. I can't help it. It's a cute outfit."

I leaned forward and kissed her softly. "You look wonderful." She moaned, and I placed my hand on her hip, squeezing slightly. "Seriously, fucking edible." I bit her lip, and she moaned again, wrapping her arms around my shoulders. Her small handbag hit me upside the head, and we both laughed as I rubbed the spot she had hit and jokingly staggered back.

"Well, then. I see how it is."

Paige giggled. "Oops. Sorry. You know this is our fourth date now. Or fiftieth. Depending on how you think about it. You'd think we'd be better at it."

"I like the idea of it being our fiftieth." I put my hands in my pockets to avoid reaching out to undo the tie at her waist. I knew the dress would fall to the sides, baring her to me. And all I wanted to do was put my face between those massive breasts of hers and have way too much fun.

I was a horrible person, and from the way her gaze darkened as she looked at me, she knew what I was thinking.

"Dinner first. Dessert later."

I groaned, gripping myself over my pants as she laughed. "You are not a good person."

"What? Are you going to be able to drive with the hard-on?"

"I could make a stick shift joke, but I'm not in the mood."

She walked down the stairs, and I slapped her ass. "Hey!"

"What? It was right there. I couldn't help it."

"You are a problem, Lee Grier. Just saying."

"I don't mind. If you walk in heels like that in front of me, I will have to grab your ass. It's just how things go."

"I don't mind." She fluttered her eyelashes, and I kissed her hard on the mouth, unable to stop.

"If you aren't careful, we aren't going out. We're just going right back inside."

I groaned. "Do we need to eat dinner?" As if on cue, her stomach growled, and I laughed. "Sounds like we do. Come on. Let's get you fed."

"That wasn't embarrassing or anything."

"You already said that you're increasing your calories to keep up with breastfeeding. You're fine."

"And this is a lovely conversation for a date."

"I don't mind. I like knowing these things."

"I brought my pump, by the way," she said as she waved her bag. "Not just my handbag, but this one. I'll keep it in the car, but you know, just in case. We don't need an accident at dinner."

"That's pretty smart. Would you pump in the car?"

She shrugged. "I don't know. I'm not good at this whole multitasking thing."

"Now that's a lie."

I closed the door behind her and moved around to the driver's seat. I leaned across the center console, kissed her softly, and as she grinned at me, I pulled away, and we made our way to the restaurant.

It was a little French bistro. One where we could indulge in all the baguettes and salted butter we wanted —just enjoy ourselves. It was a new place that had popped up in the city recently, and while Paige and I tended to go to barbecues or Japanese restaurants up here more often than not, this sounded like a nice place to relax.

"Oh," she whispered as she walked in.

"What's wrong?"

"Nothing. I just…I think one of Colton's friends owns this place."

I cursed under my breath. "Shit. I didn't even think about that. I mean, I knew it wasn't the place he used to run, but I didn't realize."

"No, it's fine. It's hard to throw a rock and not hit one of those places. It's a small chef community up here. It's growing by leaps and bounds, but Colton knows a few people."

"We can go."

"Are you kidding me? I didn't come here before because of Colton, but he's not going to keep me away from what I hear is an immaculate filet."

"Damn. Now I want a filet."

"What were you going to get?"

"Not sure. Snails?"

"I love escargot. And you can't blame me."

"You're right. And frogs' legs. When I went to Paris right after college on a school trip for my research grant, I swear I tried every single little thing that would have grossed me out as a kid and loved them all."

"I'm not a huge fan of foie gras," Paige said as we moved in. "Though I should have probably whispered that in this restaurant."

"I'm not a huge fan of it either. Don't worry. We won't get it."

"Good, but we are getting the snails."

"With extra butter, of course."

"It's the only way to eat it."

"So, you're not going to mind me kissing you after we eat snails?" I said, wincing as I did.

She just beamed. "I think it'll be fine as long as we eat a filet in between."

"And butter. Lots of butter, and baguettes, and maybe a French pastry."

"And now I'm starving. Seriously."

The hostess sat us at our table, and though we didn't drink wine, we did have sparkling water and iced tea.

The food was decadent, and we did indeed share an order of snails, two loaves of bread, and the best steak I've ever had in my life.

"That's it. This is our place. We're going to have to come here for every anniversary."

"Oh, yes. I mean, we're going to have to work overtime to afford it every time, but it'll be worth it."

I shook my head. "The prices aren't as bad as they are in downtown Denver. We're fine."

"True, although it feels weird to be out here without Emery. You know?"

"I know." I squeezed her hand. "And, not to ruin the moment before we head to our next place, but I need to tell you something."

Her eyes widened. "What's wrong?"

I swallowed hard. "I may have a stalker."

She froze. "Excuse me?"

I quickly explained about the notes and the flowers and the chocolates, and her eyes narrowed with each additional thing.

"You called the cops? And my brothers know? And you didn't tell me?"

"Every time I was ready to, something happened or came up. And I couldn't put that burden on you. Nothing has happened since the roses. I just... I didn't want to have that between us. Or between you and your brothers. I swear I didn't mean to keep secrets from you. It just happened."

"Lee. Are you okay? Are you safe? Is Emery safe?"

"You have a security system. So do I. So does every single one of your family members. Anyone that will ever have Emery has a security system. And all of the guys plan to tell their spouses tonight about it. Benjamin is making sure."

She met my gaze, worry filling them, and then sighed. "Well, I'm glad. But, hell. That's scary. Especially with what happened with Annabelle."

I nodded, my stomach twisting. "I know. But nothing's come of it. There's no evidence that the person's dangerous or that something's going to happen, but we *are* keeping a lookout. I should have told you. But then the baby, and Colton, and the water main break, and work, and it just…there are no excuses other than I'm sorry. But I'm telling you now."

Paige bit her lip and nodded tightly. "Okay. So, I know. And I'm just glad you're okay. But it's scary."

We had already paid the check, so I stood, walked around the table, and gripped her hand. I pulled her up and kissed her softly. Somebody clapped gently nearby, and I smiled against her lips. "Let's get out of here. I just want to hold you."

"Sounds like a plan."

She grabbed her bag, and we walked hand in hand out of the restaurant. It felt right. Real. But a darkness surrounded us, and the unknown of what could happen was always there. But I couldn't focus on that. Wouldn't. Not with Paige in my arms. We would be safe. There was nothing else to do.

"Your place or mine?" I asked, my voice a growl. "Or Annabelle's."

"Yours. Let's go to yours. I don't get to see your place often."

"Okay, then. For more dessert? I think I have some cake. Or I can make one."

"I'm sure Brenna could deliver us a cake in a minute. However, I just want to be with you. Okay?"

I adjusted myself again and drove as quickly as I could without breaking the sound barrier. Paige was laughing as I pulled in, the tires screeching, and then our hands were all over each other. Somehow, we made it out of the car, into the garage, and stumbled into the house. She tugged on my shirt, and I unwrapped her dress. And just like I'd imagined, it fell to the floor, and she stood there in heels, her breasts overflowing her lacy bra, and her panties a bare scrap of lace.

"My boobs are far too big for this bra right now. Just saying."

I undid the clasp and pulled the cups away, her breasts falling heavy. She moaned, cupping herself. "My nipples are so sensitive."

"Just tell me if it's too much. I don't want to hurt you."

"Just be gentle. And maybe no sucking on them. That might be a little too much for me."

I swallowed hard and ran my thumb over a nipple. It puckered, and she winced.

"Okay, no breast play."

"Sounds like a plan to me." I lifted her into my arms and cradled her to my chest, carrying her to the bedroom. I sat her in the middle of the bed, and she wrapped her arms around her stomach, blushing.

"I haven't, well, you know. You're the last person. And yet, this feels weird."

I gently removed her arms from her stomach and spread my hands over her belly, over the stretch marks that had come from Emery.

"You made a baby. You are as gorgeous now as you were before. I promise you. I love your body, Paige. I always have, and knowing how incredible you are now? I love it even more. Don't hide yourself from me."

"Easier said than done."

"Then I guess I'm going to have to do my best to

make sure you know exactly what I feel." I toed off my shoes, stripped off my shirt, and knelt between her legs. She still wore panties and those damn heels I imagined digging into my back, so I pulled her to the edge of the bed and let out a soft breath on her pussy.

She bucked off the bed, but I held her down softly, my hands on her hips as I nuzzled her with my nose. She still wore the lace, and when I pushed it to the side, I found her wet and swollen for me.

"Just be gentle. I know the doctor gave me the go-ahead, but this is still my first time."

"I feel like it's my first time, too," I whispered and then licked and sucked. She groaned, her thighs clamping around my head as the two of us moaned. She arched, and I spread her, lapping at her clit, spreading her folds. And when she came, she let out a slight sound that went straight to my groin. She clamped around my finger, but I was gentle, easing her into another orgasm, taking in her pleasure as much as I could.

I stood up then, removing her shoes and her panties before doing the same with my pants.

"Condom," she muttered, and I nodded.

"Oh, yes. Condom."

I gripped the base of my cock, stroking myself, once, twice. Paige slid her hands between her legs, playing with herself as I did the same. She bit her lip, her body blushing beautifully as she brought herself to another orgasm. I held mine off. I quickly slid the condom over my length and then rolled us over, positioning her on top of me.

"You set the pace, baby."

"I've already come too many times. I don't think I can do it again."

"Then ride me. And make me come. Do you think you can do that?"

"I think it sounds like a dare."

And then she slid on top of me, her pussy gripping my cock like a vise, and we both let out a shocked gasp.

"Were you always this big?" she squeaked.

"I don't know. Were you always this fucking tight?"

I struggled to concentrate, my hands tightening on her hips.

"Focus," I grumbled.

"Are you talking to me or you?"

She leaned over me, and I did my best not to touch her breasts. I didn't want to hurt her, so I slid my hands over her backside, gripping her ass, and I thrust up. She let out another shocked gasp, and I took her mouth.

And then we were moving, both of us slightly clumsy at first as we learned each other's rhythms, but I couldn't breathe, couldn't focus. And when I moved us to the side, lifting one of her legs over my hip, I slid deeper inside her, needing her. Her nails scratched down my back as I kept one hand on her hip and thigh, the other on the back of her neck, angling her so I could kiss her deeper. And then my balls tightened, the base of my spine tingling, and I came, filling the condom and whispering Paige's name.

We lay against one another, both of us sweaty and tired, and I just smiled at her.

"Whoa," she whispered.

"That's a fucking good word."

"I feel like that was a first time and yet a hundredth. And I only wish we could have been doing that for as long as we've been together and yet not together."

I brushed her hair from her face, kissing her gently.

"I'm glad that we can at least practice now. You know, because practice makes perfect."

"Sounds like a plan."

I slid out of her, took care of the condom, cleaned us both up, and then held Paige close as our hearts finally slowed down.

"I need to pick up Emery," she said after a moment, and I nodded.

"I'll drive you."

"I hope so, since you have the car."

I laughed, squeezing her hip.

"Will you stay the night?" she whispered. I froze marginally before I let out a relieved breath.

"I thought you'd never fucking ask."

"Good. Because I want to wake up with you, Lee. I

want you there in the morning while we figure out what we need to do, and you can help with those late-night feedings."

"Sounds like a plan. I'm actually quite excited to see Emery at night."

"And not to cuddle with me?"

"Well, we know my priorities."

She laughed, and then I kissed her again. We got dressed and headed towards her daughter. The little girl that had control of my heart. The one I knew I would always have in my life.

Now I just had to convince her mom of that notion.

And, frankly, a little bit of myself, too.

CHAPTER 17

Lee

"I'm not sure we have enough food," Austin Montgomery said from the kitchen, his hands on his hips. His son, Leif, stood by him and snorted.

I walked up next to them, looking at the spread before them as I shrugged. "I suppose we can always order more wings."

"Do we need more wings?" Jacob asked as he walked into the kitchen with us, his phone in his hand. "I can do it."

"I hope that y'all are kidding," Archer said, rubbing

his stomach. "I'm not supposed to gain weight right after the wedding. What is it, the honeymoon fifteen?" he asked with a wink, and I rolled my eyes.

"You work out more than I do. I think you're fine. Plus, if you did gain weight after the wedding, that just means you're hanging out with your husband more. There's nothing wrong with that."

Archer grinned at me, and Beckett walked into the room, Benjamin behind him. "I think you hanging out with Paige as much as you do is really helping your sensitive side."

"I'm going to have to hurt you, aren't I?" I grumbled.

"Don't do it," Benjamin warned as he slid out of the way.

Eli, Eliza's older brother, walked in behind him and stared at us. "Is there a reason we're all hanging out in the kitchen, looking at the food and not eating?" the large man asked. Eli was built like a tank and could probably break me with his pinky just like Andrea's husband could. I knew Eli had just gotten out of the military and probably didn't need to keep in as good of shape as he was, but that didn't seem to stop the man. If anything, he looked fitter than he had before. Hell, maybe I needed to go to the gym more often.

Archer caught my look, and I groaned. "What?"

"You're thinking about going to the gym because we

have new flesh in our group. And you're no longer the prettiest one here."

Leif snickered. "You thought you were the pretty one?" the kid asked, and though he was nineteen now and not quite a kid anymore, he was still the next generation.

"You should be nice to your elders, son," I growled.

"Don't call me an elder," Austin stated as he put his arm around his son's shoulders. "I'm having a hard enough time with the fact that he's going off to college soon."

"You had an extra year with me. You should be fine. We've prepared for this. I would be more worried when Colin goes to college. That means *I* am therefore old."

The rest of us groaned. "If you get to call yourself old, then I am one foot into the nursing home," Eli growled. "Let's not make it an issue. Shall we?"

I shook my head, then grabbed a platter of wings. "Let's go put this all on your dining room table, Jacob. It's closer to the TV so we can watch the game."

"It's going to be a shitty game," Jacob grumbled. "I don't know how many times we can have a losing season and still call us a professional football team."

"Don't say things like that. It's not good for our self-esteem." Archer hip-checked Jacob slightly, and we all made our way into the dining room, setting down the platters of food before plating up snacks for ourselves and heading to the living room for pregame.

We all took our seats in the living room, some of us on the floor, others crammed onto the couch, but it was comfortable. A guys' evening. One that didn't include the bar or going around town. Maybe this was the next stage of life, but I didn't give a shit. It was nice. And, frankly, I was exhausted.

"Is Clay out with Riggs?" Archer asked as he bit into his wing.

"Riggs had to work tonight, so Clay thought he would join him. The kids are with Annabelle and Eliza."

I looked over then. "Really?"

"We're all trying out this swapping kids thing. It's working so far," Jacob added with a shrug.

"Is Marc out of town again?" Austin asked before taking a bite of his dinner.

Archer nodded. "Yep. But he should be home tomorrow. Which is two days earlier than planned. And let me tell you, I am tired of phone sex." He blushed. "Sorry, Leif."

Leif just held up his hand. "Oh, no, it's fine. Phone sex is okay, but I guess the real thing's better."

Austin put his hand over his face and groaned. "You guess? No, I don't really want to know. When did you get old enough that we could have this conversation?"

"When I was twelve, and you told me about the

birds and the bees? Or when I was going on my first date, and you handed me a condom, not knowing that Mom had already done so? Or maybe it was prom when you both sat me down and explained to me that enjoying the night meant enjoying consent, safety, and not growing up too quickly."

I burst out laughing, as did the others, and Austin just groaned. "That reminds me, I guess we're going to have to do this all over again. Three fucking times. Four kids. How did I end up with four kids?"

"Do we need to have the birds and the bees talk with you, too?" Archer asked with a laugh.

"Plus, I'm pretty sure the rest of your siblings are ending up with even more," I teased.

Austin sighed. "True, of course, you and Paige over there have a little bit of time before you have to deal with that. How is Emery?"

"Freaking fantastic. I have pictures." I pulled out my phone and grinned.

Eli gave me a sharp look. "You and Paige, then? Interesting."

I scowled at the other man. "What's so interesting?"

"What? I like it. The Montgomery girls are hot. You know Annabelle used to date Elliot," Eli added, speaking of his brother.

"I do, but I don't know why you're bringing it up now."

"This is fascinating," Leif said and let out an *oof* as Austin elbowed him in the gut.

"Anyway, you and Paige are dating?" Eli asked.

I shrugged. "Yes. You got a problem with that?"

Eli held up both hands. "I don't. Hell, I'm glad that she is dating you rather than that asshole who left her."

"Do not get me started on him," Beckett growled before biting into a nacho.

"Yes, let's not get started," Archer stated.

Eli shrugged. "Anyway, you guys are perfect for each other. I'm happy. Plus, I know that you've been around for this whole pregnancy thing and for Emery. Sounds good to me. Not that my opinion matters."

"Eliza sure does tell you a lot," I said with narrowed eyes.

"Sometimes. Other times, I have to pry it out of her. Mostly, I want to know how that big oaf over there is treating her."

Beckett leaned forward. "You may know how to kill a man with one hand, but I could still take you out. Just saying."

Eli winked. "Not nice to threaten the brother-in-law."

I laughed at the play-by-play, as everyone began eating in earnest. I leaned back and rubbed my stomach. "I'm going to have to work out twice as hard tomorrow. Maybe next time we do salads?"

"We did salads last time," Benjamin put in but sighed. "Maybe soup. Or stew. No more grease. I think we're too old for grease."

"I like it," Leif said with a grin as he devoured another wing. I bundled up a napkin and threw it at the kid's head, but Austin caught it.

"Don't throw things at my kid. Only I can throw things at my kid. And, Leif? Stop showing off how young you are and how much prowess you have. It's not nice. Not with us old people who are thinking about arthritis medication."

"My knee has been acting up," Archer added. "It must be the rain."

I snorted. "You're in your twenties. Shut up."

"So are you."

We ate a little bit more and watched the game, and I looked around at my friends and figured that…yeah, I'd done pretty well for myself. There was still the unknown out there, the person who had left the notes, but they hadn't done anything recently, so I figured that maybe that would be the end of it. We were all just hanging out and enjoying ourselves. Later, I would go home alone, but I would see Paige tomorrow. Only I didn't want to go home. I wanted to go to Paige's. I wanted to have the right to have that be my home. But I knew it was too soon. Just like it was too soon to tell her that I loved her.

"What's with the serious face?" Eli whispered as the others cheered on a particularly good play.

"What? I'm just thinking."

"About Paige?" Eli asked, his head tilted.

"Maybe. I don't know. We did things a little backward."

"I feel that," Eli said, plucking a piece of lint off his jeans. "But sometimes it's the only way."

Confused, I turned to the other man. "How are things in Texas?"

"Different. Hard. Easy. Everything." The other man shrugged. "It's just the way things are. I don't know. We're figuring it out, though."

"And all of you decided to move down there?"

Eli nodded. "All of us but Eliza. I figured she would want to move down with us, but then she fell in love with a Montgomery, and now she's stuck in Colorado for the rest of her life."

I knew Eli was teasing as he said it, but I nodded. "When you fall for a Montgomery, you're sort of stuck with the whole family. Not that it's being stuck."

Eli smiled. "I don't think there's a single Montgomery for me, so it looks like I'm going to have to go outside of that family pool."

"True," I added with a laugh. "Plus, you're just settling in Texas. You don't want to have to move back up to Colorado."

"Probably not. But it's nice to see my sister and just relax for a bit. Benjamin hardly lets me do any home repairs at the house since he's a master at it, but I can pretend that I'm helping my baby sister."

"What are we talking about over here?" Archer asked as he leaned into us.

"Family," we both said at the same time, and I laughed, Eli joining in.

Archer grinned. "It's nice to have us all here. It's good to be able to just take some time off."

I looked at Archer, wondering at the strain in his eyes, but I didn't ask. He would tell us when he needed to. Or we'd all give up waiting and rip it out of him. From the look on Eli's face, maybe there was something we needed to tear out of Eli, as well. But for now, I let it be and listened to my friends talk while watching the game. I told myself that tomorrow I would see Paige and Emery.

I could take a night off. And maybe I should. Because falling this hard and so fast? It couldn't be good. I didn't want to hurt them or me. I would take the time. Center myself and not want what I couldn't have.

CHAPTER 18

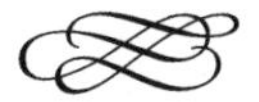

Paige

"When was the last time we had a girls' evening, with no babies, no husbands, boyfriends, or screaming?" Brenna asked as she rolled her shoulders back, leaning into the couch.

Mom sat next to her and grinned. "I love having an empty nest, but I also hate it. This is why we have so many dinners at our house."

"Is Dad at home alone, then?" I asked, taking a sip of my iced tea.

"No, he's out with Beckett and Clay, dealing with something on the job site."

I frowned and picked up my phone to look at our work calendar. "Did I know this?"

"You're technically still on maternity leave," Annabelle singsonged.

I shook my head. "But I'm not. I mean, I should be kept in the loop."

"It's not on the docket. Your father just wanted to see the job site because he misses it, not to give any advice unless asked," Mom added quickly, and I smiled.

Things had been difficult in the past with how they'd handled leaving the company—or rather how they hadn't left like they said they would. But things were much better now, and I was grateful for it.

"I'm just glad we could all be here together," Mom said after a moment and squeezed my hand.

"I'm glad you're here, too. Although, I don't know if you came here for Emery or me." I looked at the baby monitor and saw her still sleeping in her little bassinet, the screen in black and white since the lights were turned off.

"While I appreciate the fact that she needs to nap, she should know that her grandmother is here and wants to hold her. And you won't let me pick her up and walk her around the house."

I rolled my eyes as my sisters laughed. "Because you never wake up a sleeping baby. You taught me that."

"It's true, because then Emery will be up for the rest

of the day and into the evening, and you will never sleep again," Annabelle added as she reached for a cupcake. "Seriously, Brenna. Stop bringing over cupcakes."

My sister-in-law shrugged. "That's a cornbread cupcake. It's savory. It's yummy."

"Oh, I'm sure it is, but I'm going to be so full of every type of cupcake you make that I'm never going to be able to get out of this chair."

Brenna just grinned. "I can't help it. I'm that good of a baker and cake decorator."

And she was. Each cupcake was elegantly decorated with frosting and toppings and looked as if it were from a patisserie. I was so grateful that there were so many talented people in my life. Except for the fact that I was going to burst from the number of cupcakes I had consumed recently.

"I never would've thought to make savory ones with cornbread and other types. It's genius." Mom leaned forward, plucked a cornbread muffin from the tray, and took a bite. "Seriously, delicious. I'm so glad that Beckett married you. Not just because you bake for me, but because you are a wonderful daughter to add to my collection."

Annabelle and I burst out laughing.

"Collection?" I asked, wiping away a tear. "Is that what you are? A collector?"

"I picked up Eliza and Brenna. That's two special daughters. And I also got Jacob and Marc out of the deal." She looked at me and winked. "And who knows, I might get Lee, as well."

I blushed and cleared my throat. "Mom. We're not… It's still way too early for things like that. We already know I jumped the gun when it came to Colton. I don't want to be that person again."

Mom's face sobered, and she squeezed my hand again. "I'm sorry. I was just teasing. However, do not use Colton as a yardstick." Her eyes darkened. "That little fucker abandoned his daughter, abandoned *my* daughter, so he can rot in hell for all I care. He is not who you judge others against. It is unfair to Lee and every other human being out there to do so. Do you understand me, young lady?"

Annabelle clapped, Eliza and Brenna joining in. "Hear, hear," Annabel added.

"I'm not using Colton as a yardstick," I lied. "Seriously, though, Lee and I are just beginning our relationship."

Annabelle waved me off. "You guys were practically dating throughout your entire pregnancy, even if you didn't say so."

Eliza nodded. "Lee wasn't seeing anyone else, you weren't, and you spent all of your free time together.

I'm pretty sure you are nearly a year into whatever type of relationship you thought you had."

I looked down at my hands. "I don't want to force Lee into something he's not ready for."

My mom leaned forward. "But what are *you* ready for, Paige?"

I looked up at my mom and swallowed hard. "I'm ready for cupcakes, and to be the best mom I can possibly be, and to make sure Montgomery Builders kicks ass. I don't want to put too much pressure on what I have with Lee. Okay?"

The girls looked at each other and then at me before nodding and changing the subject to the upcoming expansion. We would soon be adding a whole other set of team members to Montgomery Builders, as well as an actual expansion to the office. We redid the space and had the funds to do so. We were taking on more and more clients and being safe and cautious about it simultaneously. We didn't want Montgomery Builders to go under, so we were focusing on what we could. And that meant doing the best we could while taking care of our family and company.

Our girls' time ended, my sisters left, hugging me tightly, and my mom kissed my forehead. "Enjoy yourself. I see how you look at Lee, and the way he looks at you. You two might be thinking you're taking it slow and doing your best to focus on who you are, but don't run and hide when things get difficult. And don't bite your nose off to spite your face. You understand me, young lady?"

I nodded. "I do. However, we're going to find our own pace. Not the one others need us to take."

"Okay, baby girl. Just be safe." She kissed my cheek once again and then left me alone.

Emery let out a little cry, and I ran towards her room. I didn't always run as quickly as I did at Emery's cries of waking up. However, I needed to hold my baby.

I picked her up, looking at that wide smile, and held her close. She was still so tiny but was growing by leaps and bounds every day. I sat in the rocker, undid my button-up shirt, and pressed the baby to my breast. Emery fed quickly, and I sighed, rocking, wondering exactly how this was my life. Nothing had gone as planned, not a single thing, and yet I couldn't hate it. Because I had my daughter, I was a mom. I was damn good at my job.

And I was in love with one of my best friends. And maybe, just maybe, he could love me back.

"Knock, knock," Lee said from the door, and I started, looking up at him.

"I didn't know you were coming over," I whispered and adjusted Emery.

Lee shrugged and moved into the nursery, sitting on the ottoman in front of me. "I told you I might stop by for dinner. But from the looks of the kitchen and all the leftovers in the fridge, you guys might have already eaten."

I laughed. "We had a very filling lunch. I don't know if I could eat dinner."

"Not a problem. Mind if I eat some leftovers then?"

"I don't mind, Lee." I let out a breath, knowing I needed to stop being a coward when it came to him. "I'm glad you're here."

He smiled, leaned forward, and brushed a kiss to my lips and then to Emery's head. My heart did that little twisting thing, telling me that I should say something. Tell him how I felt. But I had tried with Colton and had failed spectacularly. I didn't know if I could fail with Lee. I didn't know who I would be if that happened. I wasn't ready.

But I needed to find a way.

"Are you sure about this?" I whispered, the words coming out of my mouth before I even realized it. Lee blinked and leaned back, sitting on the ottoman again.

"Sure about what?"

"About me. About this. About what we're doing."

He tilted his head, studying me. "I've been sure for a while, Paige. What's not to be sure about? I've been here every step of the way. I'm not going anywhere."

It wasn't a declaration of love, but it was close. It was something.

I just needed to focus. To breathe. Because I had fallen in love with Lee. But I didn't know how to tell him that. Or when the right time would be.

"Do you want me to take care of Emery while you clean up?" he asked, and I blinked, realizing that I had been staring at him and not saying anything.

I cleared my throat. "Okay. Thank you."

"It's really selfish. I just want to hold her. I like her."

"I like her, too." I handed my daughter to Lee, knowing that she was in the safest hands possible, and cleared my throat. "I'm glad that you're here for her because I trust you implicitly. With her." *With me.*

He smiled then, his eyes growing warm. "I love this kid, Paige. I loved her from the first moment I met her. It's probably a little insane, but I can't help it. She's amazing."

My heart burst again. "She is. And you've always been here, and I appreciate that."

He frowned. "Appreciate."

I swallowed hard, then kissed him again. "I'm going to say something. And I'm trying to be brave. But I don't want you to leave as soon as I do."

His expression shuttered, and he nodded tightly. "Okay."

"I love you. I've loved you for probably longer than I care to admit. But I do love you. And I know it might be too soon, or not soon enough depending, but I'm glad that you're in my life. And not just because of Emery. Because of you. So, yeah, I love you. And I have no idea what to do with that."

Lee looked down at Emery in his arms as he burped her and then leaned forward and kissed me softly. "You are so fucking brave," he whispered.

My stomach lurched, and I didn't know what he was going to say. *Brave?* What did he mean by that?

His eyes darkened. "I love you, too, Paige. I didn't mean to fall in love. I *shouldn't* have fallen in love. You know that. I told myself I wouldn't. But here I am. In love with my best friend's little sister. My best friend, too."

Tears fell from my eyes, and I went to my toes, kissing him softly. "I messed up before. I don't know what I'm doing when it comes to relationships. I don't want to be the one who screws this up."

"You aren't. I'm not. I've never had a serious relationship. I have no idea what I'm doing."

"I thought I was in a serious relationship, and I clearly wasn't before, so I don't know what I'm doing."

"Well, good. We can figure it out together. Now, I'm going to burp and change this little one, and then you and I can go have sex in the kitchen."

I blinked. "What?"

"Or in the living room. I'm not sure. Where haven't we had sex before?"

"Lee!"

"What? We just said we loved each other for the first time. Aren't we supposed to have sex? I don't know. I've never told anyone that I loved them before. Other than Emery, of course. She is the first girl I ever said that to."

I melted. Right then and there, I fucking melted. "Damn it. Why do you have to say things like that?"

I wiped tears away, and he kissed me soundly. "Go find a place. I'll take care of Emery."

"Lee, darn you. You are way too good for me."

He cursed under his breath, shaking his head. "No. Let's just say we're good for each other because I have never been with someone like this before. Have never loved someone like this. You say you fucked up with Colton? And I fucked up with everyone else. Let's not make that mistake again."

I watched him burp my daughter, the one he had been here for the entire time, and told myself that maybe this could work out. Maybe I wouldn't screw this up.

I left them alone, heading to the kitchen as I looked around for a place to make out with the man I loved. I giggled. I couldn't help it. And when Lee wrapped his arms around my waist, I leaned into him. "You really want to have sex in the kitchen?"

"Maybe not in the kitchen. But how about here?" he

asked as he nibbled on my neck. I groaned, my knees going weak.

"I thought you were kidding," I whispered.

"When it comes to having sex with you, I'm never kidding." And then he led me to the dining room and set me on the table.

"Lee! We eat here!"

"Well, then it looks like I'm going to have to eat, too." And then he went to his knees and pushed my dress up.

"Seriously?" And then I couldn't think, his mouth on my pussy as he shoved my panties to the side. I clung to the edge of the table, my knees going around his shoulders. I couldn't focus. All I could do was try not to come right there on his face as he lapped at my clit, spreading me before him. He speared me with two fingers, curling them slightly so he hit that spot he was so good at finding. Seriously, did he have a fucking map? I arched for him, pressing myself firmer against his face as he ate me out, and when I came, my knees shook, my breasts ached, and I couldn't even focus.

"I love it when you come. You get all pink and rosy, and you whisper my name in the sweetest ways."

"I am trigger-happy when it comes to you," I panted, shaking my head. "I never come like that."

"For me, you do."

He sounded so proud that I narrowed my eyes.

When I wiggled off the table, he frowned but then parted his lips when I dropped to my knees.

"We'll see who is good with their mouth, shall we?" I asked as I undid his belt. He swallowed hard, his hand going through my hair as I pulled him out of his pants. He was long and thick, and I knew exactly what he felt like in my pussy and pressing against my ass. And all I wanted to do was suck him down and give him the same pleasure he'd given me. I licked the drop of fluid at the tip, and he shuddered, his whole body going taut. And when I swallowed the crown into my mouth, hollowing my cheeks, he let out a guttural moan.

"Paige fucking Montgomery."

I looked up at him then swallowed more of him. He was too big to fit in my mouth completely, so I relaxed my throat, letting him go deeper, but used one hand on his base, the other cupping his balls as I moved, bobbing up and down as I hummed along his length. He groaned, and his whole body stiffened as if he were forcing himself not to fuck my mouth. So, I let go of his balls, gripped his hips, and moved him back and forth. He got the hint and groaned, gently fucking my mouth.

"You are sin personified, and I fucking love it." He moved harder this time, and I gagged slightly, moving back to kiss his length before swallowing him again. I hummed along him, tightening my throat muscles before he let out a shocked gasp and tugged at my hair.

"Paige," he groaned. But I didn't let him move away. Instead, I swallowed him down as he came, enjoying his orgasm because I was the one who had given it to him, just like he had done for me. And then he pulled me up, his mouth on mine as we mingled our tastes. He slid his hands under my dress, playing with my ass as I wrapped my legs around his waist.

The two of us groaned, and somehow, we made it to the living room, stripping off each other's clothes as we lay there naked, grinding against one another. He was already hard again, impossibly so, and when he slid against my heat, I froze.

"Condom."

"Fuck," he muttered. He searched around for his jeans, pulled one out of his pocket, and I laughed.

"Really?"

"I told you I was going to fuck you in the kitchen or somewhere. Of course, I brought a condom."

I nodded, took it out of the packet, and slowly rolled it down his length. When I squeezed the base of his cock, he crossed his eyes. "Jesus Christ."

"Now, do you want me to ride you, or do you want to ride me?"

In answer, he pulled my hair tightly, the sting making my pussy tighten. Then he shoved me onto my knees, my hands holding the back of the couch before he gripped my hips and pushed into me in one thrust. I let out a shocked gasp, but then he was pounding into me, my inner walls so sensitive that I almost came right there. He had one hand clamped on my hip, the other over my clit, rubbing fiercely. But then he moved that hand, pressing his thumb against my ass, and I pushed back, letting him enter me slightly. He groaned, using my wetness to make it easier. And when I came, I shouted his name, my body going weak, and he followed suit, holding me close to him as we both shuddered from our orgasms, the bliss too much to bear.

"I love you," he whispered, kissing my neck and moving me slightly so he caught my mouth.

"I love you," I whispered back.

I couldn't breathe, couldn't focus, but this was Lee. I hadn't meant to fall in love this soon. I didn't even know when it had happened.

Had it been when he held me in the rain? Or had it been when he held Emery? Or maybe it was now. I didn't know, and I didn't care. I didn't want to uncover that moment. Because in essence, Lee had always been here in some way.

I had to trust in these feelings, in this moment, and believe that he would be here forever. Or at least, for as long as forever could be in this moment. Because I had fallen in love before, but this time, it felt different. This time, it felt true.

And for once, I would let myself believe. I had to.

CHAPTER 19

Lee

"Okay, now, this is your third diaper in an hour. You're going to want to do me a solid and not do a solid. Or anything else." I looked up at Paige after I spoke, and she pressed her lips together as if trying not to laugh.

"Did you just make a joke about poop?" she asked, then held up her hands. "Nope. Because we're supposed to have an at-home date tonight, and I don't want to talk about bodily functions. We're not going to mention what you just said."

I rocked Emery back and forth as the little girl

gurgled up at me. "I can't help it. I just have a way with the ladies."

This time, Paige burst out laughing, and I rolled my eyes before walking around the nursery a bit, settling Emery down. "Do you have the recipe ready to go?" I asked over my shoulder, and Paige walked in behind me. She wrapped her arms around my waist, resting her cheek on my shoulder, and I grinned. We looked like a family. And the thing was, we were. Our own version anyway, and I didn't want to stop this. I hadn't known that this was what I wanted. What I had been afraid of. But I wasn't my father. I sure as fuck wasn't Colton. But I loved these two girls to the moon and back, and I wouldn't take them for granted.

"I do have the recipe out. However, if we mess it up, it's fine. We could just mix it all together and call it spaghetti."

I rolled my eyes and turned to kiss her soundly on the mouth before handing her Emery. "You can put her in the crib because the last time I did it without her being able to nuzzle against your breasts first, she screamed."

Paige just rolled her eyes and winked. "I thought that was you."

"I do love nuzzling your breasts. I can't help it. They're my favorite." I reached around and smacked her on the ass, then walked out of the nursery, holding back my laughter.

Paige, however, cackled before she set Emery down in the crib and followed me.

"She's just going to rest in there for a bit since she didn't sleep all that many hours last night."

I rubbed the back of my neck and raised a brow. "I remember. How the hell did you do that for the first couple of months alone?"

Paige shook her head and then pulled the Italian sausage and ground turkey out of the refrigerator. "I didn't do it on my own. Not completely. My parents were here, and then one of my siblings, and you were here practically every day. You might not have stayed the night at first, but you were here. I didn't have to do it alone."

"I'm not going to mention the C name. However, I'm still pissed off."

"I will always be pissed off when it comes to him. There will always be anger that I can't get rid of, and yet I know that he gave me Emery even if he walked away. He'll be the one to feel the pain of it. And a little part of me feels guilty about that."

I nodded and held her close. "Because we're not going to have to worry about visitation or holidays or splitting up the family."

"You said *we,*" she whispered, and I nodded tightly.

"Of course, I did. You're not getting rid of me anytime soon. Don't you get that?"

"I do. Completely. And I'm going to brush over that subject for one second only so I can say that, yes, that's why I feel guilty. Because I don't want to share her. And that makes me a horrible person. And I know that on top of all of that, I hate that Emery will never get to know Colton. That Colton will never get to know her. There's no coming back from that, and it will always be an issue that we'll have to deal with. Yes, *we*, including my family. But Emery will know that she's loved. Completely and utterly by so many people."

I let out a slow breath, gathering my anger at the man who had walked away from everything I hadn't known I craved. "And when it comes to a time when she has questions that may well happen, we'll figure it out. Together."

"Let's just hope that is what happens, and I don't burst out into tears or rage."

"If you burst out into a rage, baby, you're more than welcome to. It's your right."

"I don't want to be angry. I don't want to be sad or guilty or feel like I'm not doing the right thing. I just want to find happiness."

I kissed her soundly. "Well, let's start tonight with these lasagna roll-ups."

Paige scrunched her nose. "Mom said the regular

lasagna might be easier, but these look cuter. We can do it."

I rubbed my hands together. "I hope so. Now, we're supposed to brown the meat first?"

"From what my mom said, you cook all of the ingredients and then put it together. Some people cook lasagna raw, but that takes longer in the oven, and I don't trust us without at least watching it cook a bit."

"Exactly. And how are you supposed to roll the pasta if it's hard?"

"I'm not going to make a *that's what she said* joke because I don't think that works with that."

I snorted and kissed the top of her head. "We'll get better at the dirty jokes, Paige. However, I am a little surprised. You have three brothers, and Annabelle is great with the dirty jokes."

"I know, I know. It's like I have forgotten how to do those. I'll do better. For you."

"That's all I ask, babe."

"We'll figure it out. It can't be that hard, can it?" she asked, and I winced.

"That's literally the worst thing you could've possibly said. You've jinxed us."

She rolled her eyes, and then we got to work. It took a little bit longer than expected to make the sauce as we kept stopping to press each other against the counters, kissing and licking. It felt normal, as if we had been doing this for years rather than a few weeks, but I didn't want it to end.

I had spent the night at her house every night that week and even had a drawer in her dresser now. I had a feeling if I said the word, she'd invite me to move in, but I also didn't want to pressure her. So, we were taking our time. In our own way. But I loved waking up every morning with Paige pressed against me, the two of us making love before we quickly rolled out of bed and went to Emery.

It just felt right.

An unexpected everything.

"How's your new project?" Paige asked as we frowned at the ricotta cheese and the egg that was apparently supposed to go inside it.

"I'm excited. It's been a while since I've been able to dig into the research this way."

"So, no more papers for a while?" she asked, winking.

"Oh, probably. I hate writing. I don't know why I agreed to write the last one alone."

"Because you're good at it."

I snorted. "You say such flattering things."

She smiled, went to her toes, and kissed my cheek. "I try. Now, are you going to go to that conference in San Francisco next month?"

I looked over at her then and sighed. "That's the

plan. At least, that's what they want me to do. They'll need to buy the tickets soon, so I'll have to give them a decision."

She tilted her head as she studied me, those blue eyes curious. "Why wouldn't you?"

"I don't know. I'll be there working the entire time, and Emery's too little to travel like that, so it's not like you can come with me and make it a thing."

"You would want me to come with you on a work trip?" she asked, her eyes wide.

I shrugged, feeling subconscious. "You said you've never been to San Francisco. I'd want to show you the place. I've only been there once, but I like playing tourist."

"I would have loved to go, but you said yourself you'd be busy, and you're right, I can't travel with Emery right now. I know others can and do travel with children her age, but I don't think I'm ready for that."

"Not to mention, you have your own big project."

Paige grinned, rubbing her hands together. "You know it. I'm excited. We're breaking ground on the new office next week. And I get to start training my assistant."

She beamed, and I leaned down, kissing her hard on the mouth. "Look at you, having an assistant. You're like a grownup."

"That's exactly what I said when I was talking to Archer about it," she said with a laugh.

"Are we going to put these in the oven soon? Or should we totally have sex on the dining room table again?" she teased as she gripped my ass.

I laughed, then kissed her hard. "Honestly, let's put these in the oven, set the timer, and then go have sex on the dining room table."

"Sounds like a plan to me."

We were just setting the pan in the oven, it taking a little bit longer to do since we kept making out, when the doorbell rang.

"Are you expecting one of your siblings?" I asked, and Paige shook her head.

"Not that I know of. But they do tend to show up unannounced. I'll go get it."

I frowned, even though this was her house. "Are you sure? You can go check on Emery while I do it."

"No, finish clearing up. I've got it."

"I see how it is. You just don't want to do the dishes." I winked as I said it before she waved her fingers at me, leaving me alone in kitchen.

"I can't hear you. I'm answering the door."

I turned on the faucet, the water drowning out background noise as I cleaned one of the bowls.

"Lee!"

My skin grew cold, and I turned off the water,

rubbing my hands on a towel as I went to Paige's side at the front door. "What's wrong?"

"No one was there, but there's a rose on the welcome mat. Something's wrong."

I swallowed hard, looking at Paige. "Call the cops."

"You think it's that person again?"

"Who the fuck would leave a rose?" I took a step outside even as Paige pulled me back in. I couldn't see anybody around, but then I spotted it, the note that had blown into the bushes, thanks to a breeze.

Knock, knock.

Who's there.

Your ending.

Your ending who.

Your ending is just my beginning, but don't fret, I'll see you soon.

I cursed under my breath, even as Paige let out a gasp and ran. I followed her, my heart racing as we turned the corner in the hallway towards Emery's nursery. Paige staggered in front of me, and I barely heard her scream as my heart dropped, and my world ended.

I couldn't focus, couldn't breathe.

Because the window was open, and Emery's crib was empty.

CHAPTER 20

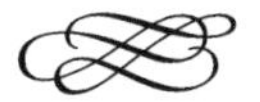

Paige

This couldn't be happening. Maybe I just couldn't see her in the shadows or something. I ran into the room, looked down at the empty crib, and screamed. "Emery! Emery!"

The window was open. How could the window be open? I had a security system. I knew it had been armed. How could Emery not be here?"

"Lee?" My voice broke, and I was one moment away from shattering completely.

"I'm calling the cops. I need to go outside and look.

Stay here." Lee's voice was so steady, I latched onto it, but there was no way I could do what he'd just said.

"I'm not going to fucking stay here. I'm going with you." I stared into those hazel-gray eyes of his as they darkened, and saw the fear and panic there that matched mine.

"Whoever's doing this could be out there. Dear God, they took her. They took Emery. Because of me."

I ignored his words because I couldn't focus on blame, not then. "We need to find her. Where's my baby?" My thoughts went in a thousand different directions as I fought to catch my breath.

How had they gotten in? How could we not have heard her? Was there more than one person? Or maybe they had been quick. I didn't know why I couldn't focus. Why hadn't I heard Emery cry out? Why didn't I hear her at all? Who had taken my child?

"Yes, someone came in and took our kid. Her name's Emery. Please, just get here."

He rattled off the address as the person on the other end spoke to him, but I needed to get out of this house. I needed to find her. They couldn't have gotten far, right? We had just put Emery down. I had seen her on the screen.

"The security camera." I ran to the kitchen and pulled up the feed, but it was static, like someone had cut the link.

I shouted, my knees going weak as I leaned against the counter, and Lee looked at me. "Whoever it is, they knew what the hell they were doing. Oh my God, I can't breathe."

"The cops are on their way," Lee said. "I'm going to look for her. Fuck, Paige."

"Maybe she's outside?" I asked, and I ran towards the back door, knowing I wasn't making the right decisions but couldn't do anything else.

"I'm using your phone, calling your brother."

Lee was good at this. He was focused. He was trying to help. And yet, I couldn't do anything. All I could do was search.

Someone had taken my baby. Someone who knew what they were doing with the security system. My mouth went dry, and my hands shook. We ran outside and searched everywhere, but I couldn't find her. There was nothing. No baby blanket. No one.

They had taken her. Right out of her nursery.

I fell to my knees, but I didn't cry. I couldn't. All I could do was try to suck in some deep breaths. And then Lee was on the ground next to me, pulling me up. He carried me into the living room. I looked up at him, trying to comprehend what was going on.

"Put me down. I can do this." He did, and I pulled my hair back from my face, using the hairband on my wrist. I couldn't break down right then. Emery needed me to be strong. That, and I needed to wake up from this godforsaken nightmare.

Lee held the phone in his hand like a lifeline, even as his skin turned gray. "Paige. I'm so sorry."

I shook my head and held out my hand. "Stop. Just stop."

He staggered back, but I couldn't tell him that I didn't blame him. Because part of me did, and yet this wasn't his fault. Someone had taken my baby.

When the sirens rang out, my heart raced, and bile filled my mouth. Two cruisers pulled up as people came out of their homes to see what was going on. I ignored the others and focused on people who could help me find Emery.

"Talk to us," one of the cops said, and we explained.

I tried to sound calm, but there wasn't anything calm about my words. "We were cooking dinner. She was just on the screen, but now the screen is blank. Someone took my baby."

"You're Paige Montgomery?"

"Yes."

"And this is the father?"

"No, the father isn't here. He's out of the picture." The cops gave each other a look, and I shook my head. "He lives in New York. This wouldn't be him."

"This is my fault," Lee put in, and the cops stared at him.

"Excuse me, sir?"

"I have a stalker. This was the same type of note. And that rose…" Lee explained what was going on, and I added what I could, though I didn't know much. All I knew was that they thought it was Colton or the stalker, and yet nobody was doing anything. People were combing through my house, searching for clues, doing whatever they could. Yet I couldn't find my baby.

Why couldn't I find my child?

"I need to breathe."

"Okay. Okay," Lee said. "We'll find her."

I met his gaze and nodded. "We have to. We have to find Emery. She'll be so scared. It's getting dark soon. She's going to be cold."

"We'll find her."

I needed to find her.

THEY HADN'T FOUND HER.

It had been nearly eighteen hours, and we still hadn't found her. The Amber Alert had gone out, and they hadn't found my child. They didn't tell me much, only that someone who knew what they were doing had blocked the security feeds and broke in. That was all they could tell us. Lee had explained everything he possibly could, and while I knew the cops didn't suspect the two of us, it felt as though we'd been interrogated and wrung dry. Considering that we had been in the home, they felt that something was hinky, and so did I.

My home was full of Montgomerys now, at least those who could leave to be with me. Others were gathered in other places together with the kids.

Why couldn't I find Emery?

"You need to sleep, Paige," Annabelle whispered.

I looked at my sister, at the tears in her eyes, her swollen features, the teeth marks on her lip, and I shook my head. "I don't think I'm ever going to be able to sleep again."

My mother was in the kitchen, cleaning the lasagna roll pan from the day before. We had burned them, causing the alarms to go off. I had nearly shuddered at the sound. A detective had helped me take the rolls out of the oven so I wouldn't burn down my home.

My baby's home.

Someone had kidnapped my child, and I couldn't do anything except stand there and wait. The authorities were searching, but thankfully, I didn't have to deal with the media. I had been warned that they might come. That I might have to give a statement to the news stations. I did not want to become a statistic. I did not want to do any of that. I just wanted my child to come home.

"I need some fresh air. I'm going to go outside. Just for a minute."

Annabelle held my elbow but nodded tightly. "We're here if you need us. All of us. I promise."

I looked at her, at Archer and Marc, at my mother and father, and swallowed hard. "Thank you. I just need to breathe. I just need to breathe."

It was a lie. It was all a lie, but I couldn't do anything else. I stood outside under an old oak tree, and leaned against the bark, facing the park that sat behind my house. It was a small piece of land, one almost hidden for my neighbors and me. I had wanted to bring Emery out here when she was older, to let her play and learn to do cartwheels and somersaults. Maybe start a game of soccer. I wasn't sure what I was supposed to do now. Why had they taken her?

"Paige?"

I whirled at the sound of Lee's voice and put my hands to my mouth. "You startled me."

He stood there, the despair on his face making me want to reach out and console him, and yet I didn't know if he would want me to.

"I love you, Paige. I'm so sorry."

I shook my head and moved forward. My back to the park. "I don't blame you."

"I sure as fuck blame me. That note was the same as

the others. It has to be whoever was doing that. But I have no idea who it was. Who it *is*. Or why."

Everything felt dull inside, as if I couldn't feel what I needed to in that moment. "I know you don't. We're going to find her."

"I know we will. We're going to find her, and we'll make sure this never happens again. I'm so fucking sorry." He let out a breath. "I should go. I should go so you and your family can deal with this. I shouldn't be here. This is my fault."

I shoved at him then and scowled. "No. You're family, too. You said you love me. Well, this is it. This is what love is. Standing together. I'm not going to have someone else walk away because it's too tough. I am barely holding on, and I need you to stay. Can you do that? Can you be strong for me? Because in the next minute, I'm going to break down, and I don't think I'm strong enough for that."

Lee cupped my face and leaned forward. "I will be whatever you need me to be. I said before that I would be here for you through thick and thin. Through all of this. But I didn't know if you wanted me here."

"I'll always want you here, Lee. That's the problem."

He didn't kiss me then, and I was glad for it only because I knew I would break down. Instead, I wrapped my arms around his waist, and he held me. Just the two of us under the old tree, the silence deafening.

A few moments later, I heard a cry and whirled, my feet moving of their own volition before I even realized I was doing it.

Lee was right behind me, and then he was passing me, the two of us running.

Emery lay on a blanket, screaming, her little fists waving in the air. I ran towards her. Lee pulled me back, and I nearly pushed at him, shoving at him, and then I realized why he'd stopped me.

A woman with dark hair, clean black slacks, a white button-down shirt, and manic eyes stared at us.

She held a knife, and I almost threw up.

"I'm sorry," the other woman said as Lee pushed himself in front of me, blocking me from her.

I tried to move past him, but he was so strong that I could only get to his side. I just needed to get to Emery. She was crying. She was hungry. My breasts ached, my milk coming in at her cries, and it was all I could do not to push Lee out of the way and reach for my baby. But that woman was so close to Emery with that knife, and I couldn't do anything but stand there and beg the gods for my baby to be unharmed and safe.

"Caroline?" Lee gasped. "What the hell. Caroline?"

He knew her. *I* knew her. I'd met her before in passing. I knew this woman. She'd dated Lee before, but it hadn't been serious, and yet here she was, holding my life in her hands. It was fate's sick joke, and I couldn't keep up with the punch line.

The woman bit her lip, her gaze glassy. "I thought you loved me. I just thought... I don't know. I know that we were so busy before, but I thought you loved me. And then you left. You left me behind."

"What?" I whispered fiercely as I stared at her from beside Lee.

Lee spoke up then, his voice calm, soothing, but I could hear the underlying panic. I just prayed Caroline couldn't. "Caroline. I'm sorry. We can talk this over. I promise. Just let me get the baby. Let me get the baby because she's hungry. Can't you see? She's hungry."

The other woman's gaze drifted, her body swaying. "I gave her formula that I got at the store. I didn't want her to be hungry. I just wanted you to notice me. Because you have a new family now, and it should've been me. Don't you see? It should've been me. But then you chose Leia. I remember Leia. She was a friend. And you dated her. But you left her, too." Caroline met my gaze. "He left me and her for you. I don't want to hurt the baby. But why doesn't he love me?"

My heart twisted, and I could barely follow her words. Emery cried out again, and I nearly pushed Lee out of the way, tears falling down my cheeks. "Please just let me hold my baby. Please. I'll do whatever you want. Just let me hold her."

"I don't want to hurt anymore."

She held the knife up, and I screamed, but then the knife clattered to the ground, far away from Emery, and Caroline fell to her knees, crying. I ran, Lee at my side, and we practically tackled each other as we fell near Emery. He picked up my baby, pressed her to me, and I sobbed, holding my daughter close. Others were shouting then, coming up from behind, the authorities and my family. They must have heard us or saw us run. I didn't know. But others were there.

And I couldn't focus on them. I could only look at my baby and hold her close. She quieted, her eyes on me as Lee held me tightly to him, and I wept.

Lee was a good man, I knew it, but something was so wrong. Not with that woman, but with everything that had happened, and I couldn't come up with the words to make things okay again.

I would never forget this, not what happened and not the feeling. And then Lee whispered that he was sorry, kissing my forehead and running his hands down Emery's body. The paramedics came forward, and I knew I'd have to let my baby go. Yet I just sat there, wondering what the hell had just happened and when I would wake up from this nightmare.

CHAPTER 21

Lee

To say I blamed myself would be an understatement.

The two days after finding out it had been Caroline all along passed as slowly as a glacier moved through time. I could not understand how it could be her.

Caroline had been nice, but she had been focused on her career. Just like I was. She had worked for a security company, and while I had thought she was the adminis-trative assistant, it turned out she had been in charge of the technology of the security systems themselves. She literally set them up for the company we had hired. She knew exactly how to get in and out without detection, and I hadn't even known she had that power. I hadn't known she'd had the skill.

She'd had a psychotic break after witnessing an attack, according to her superior. They had been apologetic, had given over any information they could about her, but hadn't realized she had gone so far over the edge. I hadn't realized that it could even be her to begin with.

Caroline had fixated on me because I had been a good part of her past, but she had never loved me. I knew that. Just like I knew I had never loved her. Paige was the only person I'd ever loved like that. And yet, I wasn't sure she would ever be able to look at me again without seeing Emery screaming on her blanket. I knew I would never forget the image for as long as I lived. Emery had been kidnapped from her crib, and I had almost lost everything that mattered.

In the days since the kidnapping, the media had gotten wind of what had happened, but we hadn't given a statement. There had been no photos, no press—at least not within the family. The articles had mentioned that a local baby girl had been kidnapped and found, and a family could sleep well at night. That was what the news had said, yet was that the case? Would we be sleeping well? I wasn't sure I could ever sleep again.

"Lee?" Paige asked from the doorway, and I realized

I was sitting in the living room, watching Emery sleep in her crib. We had moved the crib out of the nursery, as Paige wasn't sure she could even use that room again. I wasn't sure what we would do or what would happen next, but Emery was safe. After being given a full workup by her pediatrician and found to be healthy and unharmed, I'd breathed a sigh of relief. Caroline had taken good care of Emery, and yet, I wasn't sure I would ever reconcile that fact.

"I'm just watching her sleep."

"I keep doing it, too. She's so young, she won't remember any of this, but I will."

I looked at Paige and held out my hand, wondering if she would take it. When she slid hers into mine, I let out a relieved breath and pulled her to my side. She wrapped her arm around my waist and leaned into my chest. "Your family is gone, then?" I asked, and Paige looked up at me.

"They all went home for the night. I'm sure we'll see them tomorrow. And the day after. And at work, and every evening they can get away. I think they're just as scared as we are at this point."

I let out a hollow laugh. "I honestly don't know if that's the case."

She looked up at me and smiled softly, her eyes filled with tears. "Caroline is gone. She's not going to hurt this family anymore. And, honestly, knowing what she saw, what she saw that man do to that family? I understand a little."

I blinked, shocked at her words. "What? How could you—? How could you understand any of it?"

"She saw that man do horrible things and couldn't help them. She tried, but she couldn't. I understand a little bit maybe why she broke the way she did. She's not going to hurt us, and she's not going to hurt herself anymore. Emery's going to be safe, and if I ever want to sleep again and let that child out of my sight for even one instant in the next fifty years or so, I'm going to have to learn to breathe. And I'm going to have to learn to forgive."

This woman. I couldn't even fathom the heart of her. Paige Montgomery was fucking everything, and I was humbled to be in her mere presence. "I'm sorry for bringing her into our lives."

"Stop it. Just stop it." She went to her tiptoes and kissed me softly, and I nearly fell to my knees at her taste. "It's not you. It was never your fault. You are such a good man that she focused on you because you were safe. That is what the therapist said. And we will continue to go to one, Lee. I know that you have your own, but I'm going to be going to one, too. And maybe we'll bring Emery with us. I don't know. We need to talk this out because I do not want this between us for the rest of our lives. I love you, Lee. It's so scary about what happened. I am terrified that it could happen again. But I can't focus on only that, or I won't function. Yes, Emery's probably going to be strapped to me at work for the next year or so, and I don't care. However, you are safe. I'm safe. Emery's safe. Now, let's try to go to sleep."

I just shook my head, astounded even as a small kernel of hope blossomed within me. "You're so strong, Paige. How the hell are you even this brave?"

"I had to be brave the moment I found out I was pregnant. The moment I knew I was on my own and yet realized I wasn't because you were there. Because my family was there. I've had to be brave more than once, and yet you were always at my side, making sure I didn't have to do things alone. I'm going to be brave for you now. And we're going to talk about this, and we're going to figure out our next steps." She let out a breath. "But I don't think I can live here anymore."

I nodded tightly, and my gut clenched. "I was thinking about that, considering Emery is currently sleeping in the living room."

"We're going to move the crib to the bedroom, though."

"Of course."

"Good. Like I said, not letting her out of my sight."

"I'd say you could move in with me, but my house isn't big enough for the three of us."

She smiled softly. "I know. What about maybe moving into a new Montgomery build? The three of us."

I leaned down and brushed my lips against hers. "I think I can do that. I mean, I was already wondering when I could find the courage to ask if I could just stay here forever. With you. Just move in. Or maybe I would just do it quietly, and you never would have noticed."

She laughed softly just like I wanted her to, the sound a soothing balm to my scratched soul. She let out a breath, taking a step back. "I think you and I going in on this together would be good. It'd be rational and what I want. Because I love you, Lee. And Emery loves you, too."

"I love you both. Even if this wasn't exactly how I planned it."

Paige's eyes widened as I went to one knee and kissed her hand. "Paige Montgomery, help me find a house for the three of us, be my forever, and be our future. Marry me. Let me finally become a damn Montgomery."

She threw her head back and laughed wholeheartedly, the sound surprising me because I thought I wouldn't hear it again. And when she dropped to her knees in front of me, I nearly melted in rapture.

"Yes. I'll marry you, Lee Grier. And I cannot wait for you to become a Montgomery."

I winced. "Well, I really mean a Grier-Montgomery."

She winked at me and I laughed. "Oh, you said it. You're going to be a Montgomery. Sorry, that's how it works. It's binding. And you can even get the tattoo."

I reached around and gripped her hip right over where she had the Montgomery Iris tattoo. "I think I can do that. For you. I'm going to ask for one more thing, though." Nerves overtook me, and I took a quick inhale of breath.

"That you want to adopt Emery and be her daddy in truth?" Paige asked, and I shook my head, a smile playing on my lips.

"Thank you for taking my thunder."

"We need good, Lee. After so much, we need good. We'll be your family. And you'll be ours. And we'll figure out what happens next. Just you and me and Emery. I love you, Lee. I need you, and I want to be with you. Forever."

"Good. Because I'm not going anywhere. Even if I have to be a Montgomery."

She laughed, and I kissed her right when Emery woke up and started to cry. And so we stood, held our daughter in our arms, and I had to wonder exactly how this was my life. I hadn't known that this was what I wanted until I almost lost it. I would fight every day to prove that I was worthy of them, worthy of this, and worth what happened next.

Because I was going to be a Montgomery.

I was a father.

And I would be a husband.

Three things I'd never thought were in the cards for me, and yet were the only things I wanted.

So, I kissed Paige, then the top of Emery's head, and I held my girls as we planned our future, and I did my best not to only think of the darkness.

And I remembered that within each dark moment, there was light. A light to remind us of what we were fighting for and what outshone that darkness.

EPILOGUE

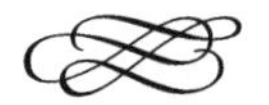

Paige

"To Paige and Lee, my best friend and my sister, I guess it had to happen," Benjamin added to his toast, and I rolled my eyes.

"Thank you for all the love. And for not beating up my fiancé." I wiggled my fingers, the diamond catching the light, and everybody clapped their hands and cheered again.

My mother held Emery close, my father behind her as they took care of their grandchild. I just sighed as Lee held me around the waist, doing my best not to move forward and pluck Emery out of my parents' arms. It wasn't going to be easy, this whole healing from the scariest moment of my life thing. I'd thought I had been scared when I almost lost Emery during the pregnancy, yet that was only a fraction of the fear I felt during her kidnapping. However, we were seeing a therapist, we were talking about it, and we were finding a home. All of this while planning a wedding and dealing with more than a few work issues. However, we were doing it. All of us.

And now we were at a Montgomery dinner and our engagement party.

I didn't need a full-on engagement party, nor would I have a huge wedding. Though the wedding would be big enough with only family. Still, I didn't need to invite the entire world. I didn't need the lavish wedding I had dreamed of as a little girl. I already had my forever, and anything else would just be icing on that wedding cake.

"So, when do we start planning?" Annabelle asked as she moved to my side. She pulled me away from Lee, who just kissed me softly before going to speak with Jacob.

"Soon. Although I thought maybe we could finish the expansion first."

Annabelle shook her head. "No, we need to focus on you."

"I feel like all we've been doing is focusing on me."

She frowned. "Not really. We've all had things going

on in our lives at the same time. It's what we're good at. So, we will plan your wedding at the same time as we plan the welcome-home party for Eliza and Beckett in a few months."

I let out a happy sigh. "I cannot wait to meet their new child."

"I can't either. You know they're excited. They've been going through a lot for this to happen, but here we are, starting our new lives. One day at a time."

I hugged my sister tight and then turned to see Eliza moving towards me.

"I heard my name. Something good?" she asked, eyes glittering.

I squeezed her and kissed her hard on the cheek. "Everything's great. We were just talking about the party we're going to throw you."

"I'm so nervous," Eliza whispered.

"You are going to be a wonderful mother."

Her eyes filled, and my heart swelled, thinking about our future. "Really?"

"If I can do it, you can do it. If I can be a mom, anyone can."

Eliza snorted. "I don't quite think that's how it works. However, we can talk about all of that soon. First, let's talk about the wedding."

I laughed. "I was so not even ready for that. You would think I would have been because that used to be all I could think about. Yet I'm happy with the way things are. You know? Maybe we can just do a Justice of the Peace thing."

"You will not, young lady. You are not depriving me of a wedding," my mom said as she held Emery, and I rolled my eyes.

"She's right. You don't get to deprive Mom of that," Benjamin called from the other room. Brenna leaned into his side, and she gave me a little wave before turning to talk to one of Eliza's brothers.

"Your brothers sure do keep visiting often," I said, knowing there was something going on there.

Eliza sighed. "They keep coming up to check on me. It's like they don't have enough going on in their lives down south."

"Meaning they have too much going on in Texas?"

"Don't even get me started. Let's just say, things are a little complicated when it comes to the Wilder brothers."

I snorted and then leaned into Lee again as he held me close. "Hello there, darling."

"Have you seen Archer?" I asked softly, and Lee's eyes shuttered.

"No. He texted Beckett and said he was going to try to make it, but something came up."

I frowned, worry settling over me. "He never misses things like this."

"I hope he's okay," Annabelle said as she played with her wine glass. "I'm really worried about him."

"I just wish he would tell us what's going on," Eliza added.

I bit my lip. "Maybe it's nothing. We're just reading too much into it. He's busy. He's a married man now."

Only we all looked at one another, an unspoken conversation happening between us. Because something was wrong with our brother, and we didn't know what it was. And now that I was trying my best not to focus on myself, maybe I would finally figure out what that was.

Lee kissed my temple. "Come on, let's go steal our daughter away from her grandmother just for a minute."

"Oh, really?" I asked, and I didn't miss the looks of glee on Eliza's and Annabelle's faces at the phrase *our daughter*. We were getting good at that because Lee was Daddy, no longer Uncle Lee or some amorphous blob that we were so good at pretending he was.

No, this was our happy ending.

Lee had always been there, and I should have seen it sooner. Maybe if I had, I wouldn't have been so heartbroken before. And yet, without Colton, without our relationship, I never would have gotten Emery. As Lee held me close and kissed me softly before placing

Emery in my arms, everyone laughed around us, and I smiled.

Colton had brought Emery into my life, and I would always be grateful to him for that. However, Lee was our future, Emery's daddy, and mine forever.

While there would always be stresses and issues and things to worry about, I wouldn't be doing them alone. I had promised myself that I would give up men, and it seemed I had failed spectacularly.

I didn't resent that in the least. Because I had my Lee. My best friend. The man I loved. A beautiful daughter.

What more did I need?

ARCHER

I swallowed hard, dread filling my gut, but I ignored the whirling emotions. I didn't have the right to be here. I had spent so long pushing everybody away because I was afraid that I'd become a ghost of myself, but I needed to do better. Everyone deserved better.

But I had nowhere else to go.

I knocked on the door, knowing it was late, the streetlights on, the chill in the air getting sharper by the minute.

I just had to hope they would answer.

My twin sister opened the door, her eyes widening. She was gorgeous with that long chestnut brown hair piled on the top of her head. She had grown it out in the past few months. I had noticed it, of course, but had been living in my own haze for so long, it was hard to focus.

Annabelle's mouth parted, and she reached for me, pulling me inside the house, the warmth almost too much for my chilled skin. "Archer? What's wrong? Why are you here? Where's Marc?"

I looked at her then and swallowed hard. "Can I stay the night?"

She cupped my face and nodded before kicking the door closed behind us. "Of course. Talk to me. Where's Marc?"

I pressed my lips together, trying to form words, only nothing came out. "I don't know. But I can't go home. I don't have my phone. I have nothing. Can I stay here?"

I was surprised that I didn't break down just then, that tears didn't fall, that I didn't shout to the world that I was nothing and useless. I'd been so good about internalizing things. Still, it was hard not to scream it.

Her eyes narrowed, and I turned slightly so I wouldn't see the judgment there. "Of course, you can stay here."

"Annabelle?" Jacob asked from the hallway. "What's going on? Archer? When did you get here?"

I looked at my sister's husband and swallowed. "I just need to stay the night, Jacob. Can I?"

"Of course," he answered, his gaze going to Annabelle. They seemed to have a silent conversation, one that I thought I'd once had. But maybe I hadn't. Maybe I had been terribly wrong.

"Of course, you can stay. Just tell me what's wrong. Do we need to call a doctor?" she asked, her voice calming.

I shook my head, giving her a small smile. "No. I'm fine. Marc and I are just getting a divorce. And I could really use a hug."

When my sister's eyes widened, and she crushed me to her in the tightest hug I had ever felt from her, I knew I would be safe. Even for the night.

Even though I was a failure. And I deserved anything that came my way.

I had thought I'd made the perfect choice.

But in the end, that choice had cost me.

And now, I had nothing.

And I wasn't sure what I was supposed to do next.

Want more Montgomery Ink?
It's time for Archer to get his HEA in INKED TEMPTATION.

Oh and yes….Leif gets a book too.

The Next Generation of Montgomerys deserve their stories beginning with BITTERSWEET PROMISES!

Want to read a special BONUS EPILOGUE featuring Lee & Paige CLICK HERE!

A NOTE FROM CARRIE ANN RYAN

Thank you so much for reading **INKED DEVOTION!**

This book took me for a ride, I'll be honest. I had no idea what was going to happen until I dove in. I love these two and their romance and I hope you did too!

And finally...after all of these years...it's time for Archer to get his HEA in INKED TEMPTATION.

Oh and yes....Leif gets a book too. The Next Generation of Montgomerys deserve their stories beginning with BITTERSWEET PROMISES!

And since we're here...yes, the Wilder Brothers get a series, beginning with Eli's book, ONE WAY BACK TO ME.

The Montgomery Ink: Fort Collins Series:

Book 1: Inked Persuasion

Book 2: Inked Obsession
Book 3: Inked Devotion
Book 3.5: Nothing But Ink
Book 4: Inked Craving
Book 5: Inked Temptation

Want to read a special BONUS EPILOGUE featuring Lee & Paige CLICK HERE!

If you want to make sure you know what's coming next from me, you can sign up for my newsletter at www.CarrieAnnRyan.com; follow me on twitter at @CarrieAnnRyan, or like my Facebook page. I also have a Facebook Fan Club where we have trivia, chats, and other goodies. You guys are the reason I get to do what I do and I thank you.

Make sure you're signed up for my MAILING LIST so you can know when the next releases are available as well as find giveaways and FREE READS.

Happy Reading!

ALSO FROM CARRIE ANN RYAN

The Montgomery Ink: Fort Collins Series:

Book 1: Inked Persuasion
Book 2: Inked Obsession
Book 3: Inked Devotion
Book 3.5: Nothing But Ink
Book 4: Inked Craving
Book 5: Inked Temptation

The Montgomery Ink Legacy Series:

Book 1: Bittersweet Promises

The Wilder Brothers Series:

Book 1: One Way Back to Me
Book 2: Always the One for Me

The Aspen Pack Series:

Book 1: Etched in Honor

Montgomery Ink:

Book 0.5: Ink Inspired

Book 0.6: Ink Reunited

Book 1: Delicate Ink

Book 1.5: Forever Ink

Book 2: Tempting Boundaries

Book 3: Harder than Words

Book 3.5: Finally Found You

Book 4: Written in Ink

Book 4.5: Hidden Ink

Book 5: Ink Enduring

Book 6: Ink Exposed

Book 6.5: Adoring Ink

Book 6.6: Love, Honor, & Ink

Book 7: Inked Expressions

Book 7.3: Dropout

Book 7.5: Executive Ink

Book 8: Inked Memories

Book 8.5: Inked Nights

Book 8.7: Second Chance Ink

Montgomery Ink: Colorado Springs

Book 1: Fallen Ink

Book 2: Restless Ink

Book 2.5: Ashes to Ink
Book 3: Jagged Ink
Book 3.5: Ink by Numbers

The Montgomery Ink: Boulder Series:

Book 1: Wrapped in Ink
Book 2: Sated in Ink
Book 3: Embraced in Ink
Book 4: Seduced in Ink
Book 4.5: Captured in Ink

The Gallagher Brothers Series:

Book 1: Love Restored
Book 2: Passion Restored
Book 3: Hope Restored

The Whiskey and Lies Series:

Book 1: Whiskey Secrets
Book 2: Whiskey Reveals
Book 3: Whiskey Undone

The Fractured Connections Series:

Book 1: Breaking Without You
Book 2: Shouldn't Have You
Book 3: Falling With You
Book 4: Taken With You

The Less Than Series:

Book 1: Breathless With Her

Book 2: Reckless With You

Book 3: Shameless With Him

The Promise Me Series:

Book 1: Forever Only Once

Book 2: From That Moment

Book 3: Far From Destined

Book 4: From Our First

The On My Own Series:

Book 1: My One Night

Book 2: My Rebound

Book 3: My Next Play

Book 4: My Bad Decisions

The Ravenwood Coven Series:

Book 1: Dawn Unearthed

Book 2: Dusk Unveiled

Book 3: Evernight Unleashed

Redwood Pack Series:

Book 1: An Alpha's Path

Book 2: A Taste for a Mate

Book 3: Trinity Bound

Book 3.5: A Night Away

Book 4: Enforcer's Redemption
Book 4.5: Blurred Expectations
Book 4.7: Forgiveness
Book 5: Shattered Emotions
Book 6: Hidden Destiny
Book 6.5: A Beta's Haven
Book 7: Fighting Fate
Book 7.5: Loving the Omega
Book 7.7: The Hunted Heart
Book 8: Wicked Wolf

The Talon Pack:

Book 1: Tattered Loyalties
Book 2: An Alpha's Choice
Book 3: Mated in Mist
Book 4: Wolf Betrayed
Book 5: Fractured Silence
Book 6: Destiny Disgraced
Book 7: Eternal Mourning
Book 8: Strength Enduring
Book 9: Forever Broken
Book 10: Mated in Darkness

The Elements of Five Series:

Book 1: From Breath and Ruin
Book 2: From Flame and Ash
Book 3: From Spirit and Binding

Book 4: From Shadow and Silence

The Branded Pack Series:

(Written with Alexandra Ivy)

Book 1: Stolen and Forgiven

Book 2: Abandoned and Unseen

Book 3: Buried and Shadowed

Dante's Circle Series:

Book 1: Dust of My Wings

Book 2: Her Warriors' Three Wishes

Book 3: An Unlucky Moon

Book 3.5: His Choice

Book 4: Tangled Innocence

Book 5: Fierce Enchantment

Book 6: An Immortal's Song

Book 7: Prowled Darkness

Book 8: Dante's Circle Reborn

Holiday, Montana Series:

Book 1: Charmed Spirits

Book 2: Santa's Executive

Book 3: Finding Abigail

Book 4: Her Lucky Love

Book 5: Dreams of Ivory

The Tattered Royals Series:

Book 1: Royal Line

Book 2: Enemy Heir

The Happy Ever After Series:

Flame and Ink

Ink Ever After

ABOUT THE AUTHOR

Carrie Ann Ryan is the New York Times and USA Today bestselling author of contemporary, paranormal, and young adult romance. Her works include the Montgomery Ink, Redwood Pack, Fractured Connections, and Elements of Five series, which have sold over 3.0 million books worldwide. She started writing while in graduate school for her advanced degree in chemistry and hasn't stopped since. Carrie Ann has written over seventy-five novels and novellas with more in the works. When she's not losing herself in her emotional and action-packed worlds, she's reading as much as she can while wrangling her clowder of cats who have more followers than she does.

www.CarrieAnnRyan.com

Printed in Great Britain
by Amazon